PENGUIN BOOKS

THE DARLING BUDS OF MAY

H. E. Bates was born in 1905 at Rushden in Northamptonshire and was educated at Kettering Grammar School. He worked as a journalist and clerk on a local newspaper before publishing his first book, *The Two Sisters*, when he was twenty. In the next fifteen years he acquired a distinguished reputation for his stories about English country life. During the Second World War, he was a Squadron Leader in the R.A.F. and some of his stories of service life, *The Greatest People in the World* (1942), *How Sleep the Brave* (1943) and *The Face of England* (1953) were written under the pseudonym of 'Flying Officer X'. His subsequent novels of Burma, *The Purple Plain* and *The Jacaranda Tree*, and of India, *The Scarlet Sword*, stemmed directly or indirectly from his war experience in the Eastern theatre of war.

In 1958 his writing took a new direction with the appearance of *The Darling Buds of May*, the first of the popular Larkin family novels, which was followed by *A Breath of French Air*, *When the Green Woods Laugh* and *Oh! To Be in England* (1963). His autobiography appeared in three volumes, *The Vanished World* (1969), *The Blossoming World* (1971) and *The World in Ripeness* (1972). His last works included the novel, *The Triple Echo* (1971) and a collection of short stories, *The Song of the Wren* (1972). Perhaps one of his most famous works of fiction is the best-selling novel *Fair Stood the Wind for France* (1944). H. E. Bates also wrote miscellaneous works on gardening, essays on country life, several plays including *The Day of Glory* (1945); *The Modern Short Story* (1941) and a story for children, *The White Admiral* (1968). His works have been translated into sixteen languages. A posthumous collection of his stories, *The Yellow Meads of Asphodel*, appeared in 1976.

H. E. Bates was awarded the C.B.E. in 1973 and died in January 1974. He was married in 1931 and had four children.

H. E. BATES

The Darling Buds of May

Piazza - Saw Gozzard
C.H.
2 - 8 - '83

PENGUIN BOOKS

in association with Michael Joseph

Penguin Books Ltd, Harmondsworth, Middlesex, England
Penguin Books, 625 Madison Avenue, New York, New York 10022, U.S.A.
Penguin Books Australia Ltd, Ringwood, Victoria, Australia
Penguin Books Canada Ltd, 2801 John Street, Markham, Ontario, Canada L3R 1B4
Penguin Books (N.Z.) Ltd, 182–190 Wairau Road, Auckland 10, New Zealand

—

First published by Michael Joseph 1958
Published in Penguin Books 1961
Reprinted 1963, 1964, 1968, 1972, 1973, 1974, 1975 (twice),
1977, 1978, 1980, 1981, 1982

—

—

Made and printed in Great Britain
by Richard Clay (The Chaucer Press) Ltd,
Bungay, Suffolk
Set in Monotype Bembo

1

AFTER distributing the eight ice-creams – they were the largest vanilla, chocolate, and raspberry super-bumpers, each in yellow, brown, and almost purple stripes – Pop Larkin climbed up into the cab of the gentian blue, home-painted thirty-hundredweight truck, laughing happily.

'Perfick wevver! You kids all right at the back there? Ma, hitch up a bit!'

Ma, in her salmon jumper, was almost two yards wide.

'I said you kids all right there?'

'How do you think they can hear,' Ma said, 'with you revving up all the time?'

Pop laughed again and let the engine idle. The strong May sunlight, the first hot sun of the year, made the bonnet of the truck gleam like brilliant blue enamel. All down the road, winding through the valley, miles of pink apple orchards were in late bloom, showing petals like light confetti.

'Zinnia and Petunia, Primrose, Victoria, Montgomery, Mariette!' – Pop unrolled the handsome ribbon of six names but heard only five separate answers, each voice choked and clotted with ice-cream.

'Where's Mariette? Ain't Mariette there?'

'I'm here, Pop.'

'That's all right, then. Thought you'd fell overboard.'

'No, I'm here, Pop, I'm here.'

'Perfick!' Pop said. 'You think I ought to get more ice-creams? It's so hot Ma's is nearly melted.'

Ma shook all over, laughing like a jelly. Little rivers of yellow, brown, and pinkish-purple cream were running down over her huge lardy hands. In her handsome big black eyes the cloudless blue May sky was reflected, making them dance as she threw out the splendid bank of her bosom, quivering under its salmon jumper. At thirty-five she still had a head of hair like black silk cotton, curly and thick as it fell to her fat olive shoulders. Her stomach and thighs bulged like a hop-sack under the tight brown skirt and in her remarkably small delicate cream ears her round pearl drop earrings trembled like young white cherries.

'Hitch up a bit I said, Ma! Give father a bit o' room.' Pop Larkin, who was thin, sharp, quick-eyed, jocular, and already going shining bald on top, with narrow brown side-linings to make up for it, nudged against the mass of flesh like a piglet against a sow. 'Can't get the clutch in.'

Ma hitched up a centimetre or two, still laughing.

'Perfick!' Pop said. 'No, it ain't though. Where'd I put that money?'

Ice-cream in his right hand, he began to feel in the pockets of his leather jacket with the other.

'I had it when I bought the ice-creams. Don't say I dropped it. Here, Ma, hold my ice-cream.'

Ma held the ice-cream, taking a neat lick at a melting edge of it with a red sparkling tongue.

'All right, all right. Panic over. Put it in with the crisps.'

Packets of potato crisps crackled out of his pocket, together with a bundle of pound notes, rolled up, perhaps a hundred of them, and clasped with a thick elastic band.

'Anybody want some crisps? Don't all speak at once! – anybody –'

'Please!'

Pop leaned out of the driving cab and with two deft backhand movements threw packets of potato crisps into the back of the truck.

'Crisps, Ma?'

'Please,' Ma said. 'Lovely. Just what I wanted.'

Pop took from his pocket a third packet of potato crisps and handed it over to Ma, taking his ice-cream back and licking the dripping underside of it at the same time.

'All right. All set now.' He let in the clutch at last, holding his ice-cream against the wheel. 'Perfick! Ma, take a look at that sky!'

Soon, in perfect sunlight, between orchards that lifted gentle pink branches in the lightest breath of wind, the truck was passing strawberry fields.

'Got the straw on,' Pop said. 'Won't be above anuvver few days now.'

In June it would be strawberries for picking, followed by cherries before the month ended, and then more cherries through all the month of July. Sometimes, in good summers, apples began before August did, and with them early plums and pears. In August and again in September it was apples. In September also it was hops and in October potatoes. At strawberries alone, with a big family, you could earn fifteen pounds a day.

'See that, kids?' Pop slowed down the truck, idling past the long rows of fresh yellow straw. 'Anybody don't want to go strawberry-picking?'

In the answering burst of voices Pop thought, for the second time, that he couldn't hear the voice of Mariette.

'What's up with Mariette, Ma?'

'Mariette? Why?'

'Ain't heard her laughing much today.'

'I expect she's thinking,' Ma said.

Lost in silent astonishment at this possibility, Pop licked the last melting pink and chocolate-yellow cream from its paper and let the paper fly out of the window.

'Thinking? What's she got to think about?'

'She's going to have a baby.'

'Oh?' Pop said. 'Well, that don't matter. Perfick. Jolly good.'

Ma did not seem unduly worried either.

'Who is it?' Pop said.

'She can't make up her mind.'

Ma sat happily munching crisps, staring at cherry orchards as they sailed past the truck, every bough hung with swelling fruit, palest pink on the sunnier edges of the trees.

'Have to make up her mind some time, won't she?' Pop said.

'Why?'

'Oh! I just thought,' Pop said.

Ma, who had almost finished the crisps, poured the last remaining golden crumbs into the palm of her left hand. Over the years, as she had grown fatter, the three big turquoise and pearl rings she wore had grown tighter and tighter on her fingers, so that every now and then she had to have them cut off, enlarged, and put back again.

'She thinks it's either that Charles boy who worked at the farm,' Ma said, 'or else that chap who works on the railway line. Harry somebody.'

'I know him,' Pop said. 'He's married.'

'The other one's overseas now,' Ma said. 'Tripoli or somewhere.'

'Well, he'll get leave.'

'Not for a year he won't,' Ma said. 'And perhaps not then if he hears.'

'Ah! well, we'll think of something,' Pop said. 'Like some more crisps? How about some chocolate? Let's stop and have a beer. Got a crate in the back.'

'Not now,' Ma said. 'Wait till we get home now. We'll have a Guinness then and I'll warm the fish-and-chips up.'

Pop drove happily, both hands free now, staring with pleasure at the cherries, the apples, and the strawberry fields, all so lovely under the May sunlight, and thinking with pleasure too of his six children and the splendid, handsome names he and Ma had given them. Jolly good names, perfick, every one of them, he thought. There was a reason for them all.

Montgomery, the only boy, had been named after the general. Primrose had come in the Spring. Zinnia and Petunia were twins and they were the flowers Ma liked most. Victoria, the youngest girl, had been born in plum-time.

Suddenly he couldn't remember why they had called the eldest Mariette.

'Ma,' he said, 'trying to think why we called her Mariette. Why did we?'

'I wanted to call her after that Queen,' Ma said. 'I always felt sorry for that Queen.'

'What Queen?'

'The French one, Marie Antoinette. But you said it was too long. You'd never say it, you said.'

'Oh! I remember,' Pop said. 'I remember now. We put the two together.'

Ten minutes later they were home. With pride and satisfaction Pop gazed on home as it suddenly appeared beyond its scrubby fringe of woodland, half filled with bluebells, half with scratching red-brown hens.

'Home looks nice,' he said. 'Allus does though, don't it? Perfick.'

'Lovely,' Ma said.

'We're all right,' Pop said. 'Got nothing to worry about, Ma, have we?'

'Not that I can think of,' Ma said.

Pop drew the truck to a standstill in a dusty yard of nettles, old oil drums, corrugated pig-sties, and piles of rusty iron in which a line of white ducks, three grey goats, and a second batch of red-brown hens set up a concerted, trembling fuss of heads and wings, as if delighted.

'Just in time for dinner!' Pop said. It was almost four o'clock. 'Anybody not hungry?'

He leapt down from the cab. Like him, everybody was laughing. He knew they were all hungry; they always were.

'Down you come, you kids. Down.'

Letting down the back-board and holding up both arms, he took the youngest children one by one, jumping them down to the yard, laughing and kissing them as they came.

Presently only Mariette remained on the truck, wearing jodhpurs and a pale lemon shirt, standing erect, black-haired, soft-eyed, olive-skinned, and so well-made in a slender and delicate way that he could not believe that Ma, at seventeen too, had once looked exactly like her.

'It's all right. I can get down myself, Pop.'

Pop held up his arms, looking at her tenderly.

'Ah! come on. Ma's told me.'

'Let me get down myself, Pop.'

He stood watching her. Her eyes roamed past him, flashing and dark as her mother's, searching the yard.

It suddenly crossed his mind that she was afraid of something, not happy, and he half-opened his mouth to comment on this unlikely, disturbing, unheard-of fact when she suddenly shook her black head and startled him by saying:

'Pop, there's a man in the yard. There's a man over there by the horse-box. Watching us.'

*

Pop walked across the yard towards the horse-box. He owned two horses, one a young black mare for Mariette, the other a piebald pony for the other kids. Mariette, who was crazy about horses, rode to point-to-points, sometimes went hunting, and even jumped at shows. She was wonderful about horses. She looked amazing on a horse. Perfick, he thought.

'Hullo, hullo, hullo,' he said. 'Good morning, afternoon rather. Looking for me?'

The man, young, spectacled, pale-faced, trilby-hatted, with a small brown tooth-brush moustache, carried a black briefcase under his arm.

'Mr Sidney Larkin?'

'Larkin, that's me,' Pop said. He laughed in ringing fashion. 'Larkin by name, Larkin by nature. What can I do for you? Nice wevver.'

'I'm from the office of the Inspector of Taxes.'

Pop stood blank and innocent, staggered by the very existence of such a person.

'Inspector of *what*?'

'Taxes. Inland Revenue.'

'You must have come to the wrong house,' Pop said.

'You are Mr Sidney Larkin?' The young man snapped open the brief-case, took out a paper, and glanced at it quickly, nervously touching his spectacles with the back of his hand. 'Sidney Charles Larkin.'

'That's me. That's me all right,' Pop said.

'According to our records,' the young man said, 'you have made no return of income for the past year.'

'Return?' Pop said. 'What return? Why? Nobody asked me.'

'You should have had a form,' the young man said. He took a yellow-buff sheet of paper from the brief-case and held it up. 'One like this.'

'Form?' Pop said. 'Form?'

Ma was crossing the yard with a box of groceries under one arm and a bag of fruit in the other. Three big ripe pineapples stuck cactus-like heads from the top of the huge paper bag. The twins loved pineapple. Especially fresh. Much better than tinned, they thought.

'Ma, did we have a form like this?' Pop called. 'Never had no form, did we?'

'Never seen one. Sure we never.'

'Come over here, Ma, a minute. This gentleman's from the Inspector of Summat or other.'

'I got dinner to get,' Ma said and strode blandly on with groceries and pineapples, huge as a buffalo. 'You want your dinner, don't you?'

Pop turned with an air of balmy indifference to the young man, who was staring incredulously at the receding figure of Ma as if she were part of the menagerie of hens, goats, ducks, and horses.

'No, never had no form. Ma says so.'

'You should have done. Two at least were sent. If not three.'

'Well, Ma says so. Ma ought to know. Ma's the one who does the paper work.'

The young man opened his mouth to speak and for a moment it was as if a strangled, startled gurgle came out. His voice choked itself back, however, and in reality the sound came from a drove of fifteen young turkeys winding down from the strip of woodland.

'Won't hurt you,' Pop said. 'How about a nice hen-bird for Christmas? Put your name on it now.'

'This form has to be returned to the Inspector,' the young man said. 'There is a statutory obligation –'

'Can't return it if I ain't got it,' Pop said. 'Now can I?'

'Here's another.'

As he recoiled from the buff-yellow sheet of paper Pop saw Mariette walking across the yard, slender, long-striding, on her way to the wooden, brush-roofed stable where both pony and horse were kept.

'I got no time for forms,' Pop said. 'Gawd Awmighty, I got pigs to feed. Turkeys to feed. Hens to feed. Kids to feed. I ain't had no dinner. Nobody ain't had no dinner.'

Suddenly the young man was not listening. With amazement he was following the progress of Mariette's dark, yellow-shirted figure across the yard.

'My eldest daughter,' Pop said. 'Crazy on horses. Mad on riding. You do any riding, Mister – Mister – I never caught your name.'

'Charlton.'

'Like to meet her, Mister Charlton?' Pop said. The young man was still staring, mouth partly open. Between his fingers the tax form fluttered in the breezy sunlit air.

'Mariette, come over here a jiff. Young man here's crazy on horses, like you. Wants to meet you. Comes from the Ministry of Revenue or summat.'

In astonished silence the young man stared at the new celestial body, in its yellow shirt, as it floated across the background of rusty iron, pig-sties, abandoned oil-drums, goat-chewn hawthorn bushes, and dusty earth.

'Mister Charlton, this is my eldest, Mariette. The one who's mad on horses. Rides everywhere. You've very like seen her picture in the papers.'

'Hullo,' Mariette said. 'I spotted you first.'

'That's right, she saw you,' Pop said. 'Who's that nice young feller in the yard, she said.'

'So you', Mariette said, 'like riding too?'

The eyes of the young man groped at the sunlight as if still unable correctly to focus the celestial body smiling at him from three feet away.

'I say every kid should have a horse,' Pop said. 'Nothing like a horse. I'm going to get every one of my kids a horse.'

Suddenly the young man woke from mesmerism, making a startling statement.

'I saw you riding over at Barfield,' he said. 'In the third race. At Easter. You came second.'

'I hope you won a bob or two on her,' Pop said.

Again he laughed in ringing fashion, bringing from beyond the stable an echo of goose voices as three swaggering grey-white birds emerged from a barricade of nettles, to be followed presently by the half-sleepy, dainty figures of a dozen guinea-fowl.

'Pity we didn't know you were coming,' Pop said. 'We're killing a goose tomorrow. Always kill a goose or a turkey or a few chickens at the week-end. Or else guinea-fowl. Like guinea-fowl?'

If the young man had any kind of answer ready it was snatched from him by the voice of Ma, calling suddenly from the house:

'Dinner's nearly ready. Anybody coming in or am I slaving for nothing?'

'We're coming, Ma!' Pop turned with eager, tempting relish to the young man, still speechless, still struggling with

14

his efforts to focus correctly the dark-haired girl. 'Well, we got to go, Mister Charlton. Sorry. Ma won't have no waiting.'

'Now, Mr Larkin, about this form –'

'Did you see me at Newchurch?' Mariette said. 'I rode there too.'

'As a matter of fact, I did – I did, yes – But, Mr Larkin, about this form –'

'What form?' Mariette said.

'Oh! some form, some form,' Pop said. 'I tell you what, Mister Charlton, you come in and have a bite o' dinner with us. No, no trouble. Tons o' grub –'

'I've eaten, thank you. I've eaten.'

'Well, cuppa tea then. Cuppa coffee. Bottle o' beer. Bottle o' Guinness. Drop o' cider.'

The entire body of the young man seemed to swirl helplessly, as if half-intoxicated, out of balance, on its axis. 'Oh! yes, do,' Mariette said and by the time he had recovered he found himself being led by Pop Larkin towards the house, from which Ma was already calling a second time:

'If nobody don't come in three minutes I'll give it to the cats.'

'Know anybody who wants a pure white kitten?' Pop said. 'Don't want a pure white kitten, do you?'

'So you were at Newchurch too,' Mariette said. 'I wish I'd known.'

A moment later Pop threw up his hands in a gesture of near ecstasy at the overpowering beauty, which suddenly seemed to strike him all afresh, of the May afternoon.

'Beautiful, ain't it?' he said. 'Perfick. I got a beautiful place here. Don't you think I got a beautiful place here, Mister Charlton?'

*

In the kitchen a radio was loudly playing jazz. In the living-room next door, where the curtains were half-drawn, a television set was on, giving to the nine faces crowded about the table a grey-purple, flickering glow.

'Have just what you fancy, Mister Charlton,' Pop said. 'If you don't see it here, ask for it. Bottle o' beer? Glass o' sherry? Pass the vinegar, Ma.'

Soon the young man, arms crooked at the crowded table, was nursing a cup of tea. In the centre of the table stood the three pineapples, flanked on all sides by plates of fish-and-chips, more coloured blocks of ice-cream, pots of raspberry and strawberry jam, bottles of tomato-ketchup and Guinness, bottles of Worcester sauce and cups of tea, chocolate biscuits and piles of icy buns.

'Perhaps Mister Charlton would like a couple o' sardines with his tea?' Pop said. 'Montgomery, fetch the sardines.'

Mr Charlton, bemused by the name of Montgomery, pro-tested faintly that he did not like sardines.

'Mister Charlton saw Mariette riding at Barfield,' Pop said.

'And at Newchurch,' Mariette said.

'Funny we didn't see you there,' Ma said, 'we was all there.'

'Mister Charlton', Pop said, 'loves horses.'

'Turn up the contrast,' Ma said, 'it's getting dark.'

In the television's flickering purplish light the young man watched the faces about the table, as they munched on fish-and-chips, ice-cream, tomato-ketchup, and jam, becoming more and more like pallid, eyeless ghouls. Pop had placed him between Ma and Mariette and presently he detected under the great breathing bank of Ma's bosom, now mauve-salmon in the flickering light, the shape of two white kittens somehow nestling on the bulging precipice of her lap. Occasionally the kittens miaowed prettily and Ma fed them with scraps of fish and batter.

Above the noise of jazz, television voices, kittens, geese hawking at the kitchen door, and the chattering voices of the family he found it hard to make himself heard.

'Mr Larkin, about this form. If you've got any difficulties I could help you fill it in.'

'All right,' Pop said, 'you fill it in.'

'It's still too dark,' Ma said. 'Turn it up a bit. It never stays where you put it nowadays.'

'I'll give the damn thing one more week to behave itself,' Pop said. 'And if it don't then I'll turn it in for another.'

Mr Charlton spread the yellow-buff form on the table in front of him and then took out his fountain pen and unscrewed the cap.

'Ma, is there any more ice-cream?' Primrose said.

'In the fridge,' Ma said. 'Big block o' strawberry *mousse*. Get that.'

'Full name: Sidney Charles Larkin,' Mr Charlton said and wrote it down. 'Occupation? Dealer?'

'Don't you call him dealer,' Ma said. 'I'll give you dealer. He owns land.'

'Well, landowner –'

'Farmer,' Pop said.

'Well, farmer,' Mr Charlton said. 'I'm very sorry. Farmer.'

'Mariette, cut the pineapple,' Ma said. 'Montgomery, go into the kitchen and fetch that pint jug of cream.'

While Mr Charlton filled in the form Mariette stood up, reached for the bread knife, and started to cut the pineapples, putting thick juicy slices on plates over which Ma poured heavy yellow cream.

'Real Jersey,' Ma said. 'From our cow.'

Every time Mariette reached over for another plate she brushed the sleeve of Mr Charlton, who either made sketchy blobs on the tax form or could not write at all.

'How many children?' Mr Charlton said. 'Six? Is that right? No more?'

'Well, not yet, old man. Plenty o' time though. Give us a chance,' Pop said and again laughed in ringing fashion.

'Gone again,' Ma said. 'You can't see a blessed thing. Montgomery, Primrose – switch it off and change it for the set in our bedroom.'

In the half-darkness that now smothered the room Mr Charlton felt something smooth, sinuous, and slender brush against his right calf. For one shimmering, unnerving moment he sat convinced that it was Mariette's leg entwining itself about his own. As it curled towards his thigh he felt his throat begin choking but suddenly he looked down to realize that already the geese were under the table, where Ma was feeding them with scraps of fish, half-cold chips, and crumbled icy buns.

Unnerved, he found it difficult to frame his next important question.

'Of course this is confidential in every way,' he said, 'but at what would you estimate your income?'

'Estimate, estimate?' Pop said. 'Income? What income?'

Montgomery and Primrose, who had carried one television set away, now brought in another, larger than the first.

'Steady there, steady!' Ma said. 'Watch where you're looking. Mind the cocktail cabinet.'

'Hear that, Ma?' Pop said. 'Income!'

Ma, as she had done in the truck, started laughing like a jelly.

'Outcome more likely,' she said. 'Outcome I should say.'

'Six kids to feed and clothe,' Pop said. 'This place to run. Fodder to buy. Wheat as dear as gold dust. Pig-food enough to frighten you to death. Living all the time going up and up. Vet's fees. Fowl pest. Foot-and-mouth. Swine fever. Birds all the time dying. Income, old man? *Income?* I should like some, old man.'

Before Mr Charlton could answer this the second television set threw across the room its pallid, unreal glow, now in a curious nightmare green. At the same moment the twins, Zinnia and Petunia, demanded more pineapple. The geese made shovelling noises under the table and Mariette, rising to cut fresh slices, suddenly turned to Mr Charlton with modest, almost whispered apology.

'I'm awfully sorry, Mr Charlton. I didn't offer you any pineapple. Would you like some?'

'No thanks. I'm not allowed it. I find it too acid.'

'What a shame. Won't you change your mind? They're nice ripe ones.'

'Ought to be,' Ma said. 'Cost enough.'

'I'm afraid I'm simply not allowed it,' Mr Charlton said. 'I have to go very carefully. I have to manage mostly on eggs and that sort of thing.'

'Eggs?' Pop said. 'Eggs? Why didn't you say so? Got plenty of eggs, Ma, haven't we? Give Mister Charlton a boiled egg or two wiv his tea.'

'How would you like that?' Ma said. 'A couple o' boiled eggs, Mister Charlton? What do you say?'

To the delight of Ma, Mr Charlton confessed that that was what he really wanted.

'I'll do them,' Mariette said. 'Three minutes? Four? How long?'

'Very light,' Mr Charlton said. 'Three.'

'Nice big 'uns! – brown!' Pop called to Mariette as she went into the kitchen, where the geese presently followed her, brushing past Mr Charlton's legs again as they passed, once more to give him that shimmering, shocking moment of unnerving ecstasy.

'About this income,' Mr Charlton said. 'Can you give me an estimate? Just an estimate.'

'Estimate it'll be an' all, old man,' Pop said. 'Lucky if we clear a fiver a week, ain't we, Ma?'

'Fiver? I'd like to see one,' Ma said.

'We want boiled eggs, too!' the twins said, as in one voice. 'Can we have boiled eggs?'

'Give over. Can't you see I'm cutting the pineapple?' Ma said.

Everybody except Mr Charlton had large second helpings of pineapple, with more cream. When Ma had finished ladling out the cream she poured the remainder of it into a tablespoon and then licked the spoon with her big red tongue. After two or three spoonsful she cleaned the spoon with her finger and fed one of the white kittens with cream. On the television screen a posse of cowboys fired thirty revolvers into a mountainside and Mr Charlton said:

'I'm afraid we have to know what your income is, Mr Larkin. Supposing –'

'All right,' Pop said, 'that's a fair question, old man. Fair for me, fair for another. How much do *you* get?'

'Oh! well, me, not all that much. Civil servant, you know –'

'Nice safe job, though.'

'Nice safe job, yes. I suppose so.'

'Nothing like a nice safe job,' Pop said. 'As long as you're happy. Do you reckon you're happy?'

Mr Charlton, who did not look at all happy, said quickly: 'Supposing I put down a provisional five hundred?'

'Hundred weeks in a year now, Ma,' Pop said, laughing again. 'Well, put it down, old man, put it down. No harm in putting it down.'

'Now the names of children,' Mr Charlton said.

While Pop was reciting, with customary pride, the full names of the children, beginning with the youngest, Zinnia Florence and Petunia Mary, the twins, Mariette came back with two large brown boiled eggs in violet plastic egg-cups to hear Pop say:

'Nightingales in them woods up there behind the house, Mr Charlton. Singing all day.'

'Do nightingales sing all day?' Mr Charlton said. 'I wasn't aware –'

'All day, all night,' Pop said. 'Like everything else in the mating season they go hell for leather.'

The plate holding the two eggs was embroidered with slices of the thinnest white bread-and-butter. Mariette had cut them herself. And now Mr Charlton looked at them, as he looked at the eggs, with reluctance and trepidation, as if not wanting to tamper with their fresh, neat virginity.

'I've been looking at you,' Ma said. 'I don't think you get enough to eat by half.'

'I live in lodgings,' Mr Charlton said. 'It's not always –'

'We want to have some of your egg!' the twins said. 'Give us some of your egg!'

'Now you've started summat,' Pop said.

A moment later Mr Charlton announced the startling discovery that the twins were just alike; he simply couldn't tell one from the other.

'You're quick,' Pop said. 'You're quick.'

'It's gone dark again,' Ma said. 'Turn up the contrast. And Montgomery, fetch me my Guinness. There's a good boy.'

Soon, while Ma drank Guinness and Pop spoke passionately again of nightingales, bluebells that clothed the copses, 'fick as carpets, ficker in fact,' and how soon it would be the great time of the year, the time he loved most, the time of strawberry-fields and cherries everywhere, Mr Charlton found himself with a twin on each knee, dipping white fingers of bread and butter into delicious craters of warm golden eggyolk.

'I hope the eggs are done right?' Mariette said.

'Perfect.'

'Perfick they will be an' all if she does 'em, you can bet you,' Pop said. 'Perfick!'

Mr Charlton had given up, for the time being, all thought of the buff-yellow form. A goose brushed his legs again. Outside, somewhere in the yard, a dog barked and the drove of turkeys seemed to respond in bubbling chorus. Far beyond them, in broken, throaty tones, a cuckoo called, almost in its June voice, and when it was silent the entire afternoon simmered in a single marvellous moment of quietness, breathlessly.

'If you don't mind me saying so,' Ma said, 'a few days in the country'd do you a world of good.'

'What are we having Sunday, Ma?' Pop said. 'Turkey?'

'What you like. Just what you fancy.'

'Roast pork,' Montgomery said. 'I like roast pork. With them brown onions.'

'Or goose,' Pop said. 'How about goose? We ain't had goose since Easter.'

In enthusiastic tones Pop went on to ask Mr Charlton

whether he preferred goose, turkey, or roast pork but Mr Charlton, bewildered, trying to clean his misty spectacles and at the same time cut into thin fingers the last of his bread-and-butter, confessed he hardly knew.

'Well, I tell you what,' Ma said, 'we'll have goose *and* roast pork. Then I can do apple sauce for the two.'

'Perfick,' Pop said. 'Perfick. Primrose, pass me the tomato-ketchup. I've got a bit of iced bun to finish up.'

'Dinner on Sunday then,' Ma said. 'About two o'clock.'

Mr Charlton, who was unable to decide from this whether he had been invited to dinner or not, felt fate softly brush his legs again in the shape of a goose-neck. At the same time he saw Mariette smile at him with intensely dark, glowing eyes, almost as if she had in fact brushed his leg with her own, and he felt his limbs again begin melting.

Across the fields a cuckoo called again and Pop echoed it with a belch that seemed to surprise him not only by its length and richness but by the fact that it was a belch at all.

'Manners,' he said. 'Pardon,' and beat his chest in stern, suppressive apology. 'Wind all of a sudden.'

'What's on now?' Ma said. On the television screen all shooting had died and two men on horses, one a piebald, were riding up the valley, waving farewell hands.

'Nobody's birthday, Sunday, is it?' Pop said.

'Nobody's birthday before August,' Ma said.

'Then it's mine,' Mariette said. 'I'll be eighteen.'

'Pity it ain't nobody's birthday,' Pop said. 'We might have had a few fireworks.'

Suddenly all the geese were gone from the kitchen and Ma, marvelling at this fact, started laughing like a jelly again and said:

'They did that once before. They heard us talking!'

'Tell you what,' Pop said, 'if you've had enough, Mister Charlton, why don't you get Mariette to take you as far as the wood and hear them nightingales? I don't think you believe they sing all day, do you?'

'Oh! yes, I –'

'Shall we ride or walk?' Mariette said. 'I don't mind the pony if you want to ride.'

'I think I'd rather walk.'

'In that case I'll run and change into a dress,' she said. 'It's getting a bit warm for jodhpurs.'

While Mariette had gone upstairs the twins abandoned Mr Charlton's egg-less plate and fetched jam-jars from the kitchen.

'Going to the stall,' they said. 'Think we'll put honey-suckle on today instead of bluebells.'

As they ran off Pop said:

'That's the flower-stall they keep at the corner of the road down there. Wild flowers. Tuppence a bunch for motorists. Everybody works here, y'know.'

'I think I passed it,' Mr Charlton said, 'as I walked up from the bus.'

'That's the one,' Pop said. 'Everybody's got to work here so's we can scratch a living. Montgomery, you'd better get off to your goats and start milking 'em.'

Presently Ma, concerned at Mr Charlton's air of retreat, uncertainty, and fatigue, spread hands like lardy legs of pork across her salmon jumper and said with earnest kindness:

'Taking your holiday soon, Mr Charlton? Where do you usually go?'

'I hadn't –'

'You should come strawberry-picking with us,' Ma said.

'Do you the world of good. Else cherry-picking. Best holiday in the world if the weather's nice. Make yourself a lot o' money too.'

'Perfick,' Pop said. 'Don't cost nothing either. Here's Mariette. Perfick, I tell you.'

Mr Charlton rose from the table to find himself stunned by a new astral body, now in a lime green dress with broad black belt, a flouncing skirt, loose neck, and short scalloped sleeves. Her beautiful dark eyes were smiling at him splendidly.

'Is that your shantung?' Ma said. 'You'll be warm enough in that, dear, will you?'

'Oh! it's hot,' Mariette said. 'It's nice to feel the breeze blowing round my legs again. You ready, Mr Charlton?'

Mr Charlton, the buff-yellow form forgotten, turned and followed Mariette, who actually stretched out a friendly hand. As they crossed a yard noisy with hawking geese, mumbling turkeys, and braying goats being led to milking by Montgomery Pop called:

'Remember about Sunday, Mr Charlton, won't you? Don't forget about Sunday.'

'You really mean it?' Mr Charlton halted and turned back, amazed. 'Are you quite sure?'

'Sure?' Pop said. 'Blimey, old man, I'm going to kill the geese any minute now.'

'Thank you, Thank you very much.'

'One goose or two, Ma?' Pop called. 'Two geese be enough? or shall we have three?'

Mr Charlton, still stunned and amazed, turned to face the waiting figure of Mariette and saw it miraculously framed against piles of junk, rampant nettles and, in the near distance, deep strips of bluebells fenced away, in the strip of woodland, from flocks of brown marauding hens. Her legs, in pale beige

25

silk stockings, were surprisingly shapely and slender. Her breasts protruded with grace from the soft lime shantung.

He could not believe in this figure. Nor, five minutes later, could he believe that the yard of nettles and junk, Pop's beautiful, incredible paradise, lay only a hundred yards away, screened by thickets of hornbeam and hazel, oaks in olive flower and may-trees carrying blossom as rich and thick as Ma's lavish Jersey cream.

'You didn't really believe about the nightingales, did you?'

'No.'

'Listen,' she said. 'You will.'

Walking along the woodland path, Mr Charlton could hear only a single untangled chorus of evening bird-song, unseparated into species, confusing as the tuning of orchestra strings.

'Let's stand here by the gate and listen,' Mariette said. 'Let's stand and listen here.'

Mr Charlton, transfixed, utterly bemused, stood by the gate and listened. Patches of evening sunlight, broken gold, sprinkled down through oak-branches, like delicate quivering translations in light of the bird-notes themselves.

'No, not that one,' Mariette said. 'That's a blackbird. Not the one over there, either. That's a wren. Now – that one. The one in the chestnut up there. The one with the long notes and then the long pause. Can you hear it now? That's a nightingale.'

Mr Charlton listened, hardly breathing, and heard for the first time in his life, in a conscious moment, the voice of a nightingale singing against a May evening sky.

Enthralled, still hardly believing it, he turned to see the deep black eyes holding him in utter captivation and heard her say again:

'You really didn't believe it, did you?'

'I must say I didn't.'

'I tell you something else you didn't believe either.'

'What was that?'

'You didn't believe about me, did you?' she said. 'You didn't believe I was the same girl you saw riding at Easter, did you?'

'No,' he said. 'How did you know?'

'I guessed,' she said. 'I could see it in your eyes. I was watching you.'

She lifted her hands and held them suddenly against his cheeks without either boldness or hesitation but with a lightness of touch that woke in Mr Charlton's legs exactly the same melting, unnerving sensation as when the geese had brushed against him under the table. A moment later he saw her lips upraised.

'Who did you think I was?'

Mr Charlton made a startling, embarrassed confession.

'I thought – well, I was actually told you were someone else in point of fact – that you were a niece of Lady Planson-Forbes – you know, at Carrington Hall –'

Mariette began laughing, in ringing tones, very much like her father.

'Now you've just found I wasn't.'

'Well, yes –'

'You feel it makes any difference?'

'Well, in point of fact –'

'I'm just the same, aren't I?' She smiled and he found his eyes level with her bare, olive shoulder. 'I'm just me. The same girl. Just me. Just the same.'

Again she touched his face with her hands and Mr Charlton took hurried refuge in a sudden recollection of the buff-yellow form.

'By the way I musn't forget to get your father to sign that form before I go –'

'You'll have to sign it for him,' she said, 'or Ma will. He can't write his name.'

She laughed again and Mr Charlton, his limbs melting once more as she lifted his hand to her bare warm shoulder, heard consciously but dizzily, for the second time in his life, a passionate burst of song from the nightingales.

At the same moment, back in the house, Pop returned to the kitchen after wringing the necks of three fat geese and poured himself a much-needed glass of beer.

'A few days like this, Ma,' he said, ''ll put a bit o' paint on the strawberries.'

Ma was raking the kitchen fire, putting on to it empty ice-cream cartons, scraps of fish-and-chips, egg-shells, pineapple tops, and Mr Charlton's buff-yellow paper.

'I don't know as I shan't get a few bottles o' port wine in for Sunday,' Pop said, 'so we can celebrate.'

'Celebrate what?'

'Well,' Pop said, 'what about Mariette?'

Ma laughed again, jumper shaking like a salmon jelly.

'The only thing is,' Pop said, 'I hope he won't want to take her away from here.' He carried his beer to the kitchen door and from there contemplated, almost with reverence, the paradisiacal scene beyond. 'Gawd A'mighty, Ma, you know we got a beautiful place here. Paradise. I don't know what we'd do if she were took away from here.'

Standing in the evening sunlight, gazing across the pile of junk, the nettles, the rusting hovels, and the scratching, dusty hens, Pop sighed loudly and with such content that the sound seemed to travel with perfect definition across the surrounding fields of buttercups and may, gathering its echo at last from the mingled sounds of the remaining geese, the voices of cuckoos calling as they flew across the meadows and the small, passionate, invisible nightingales.

'Perfick,' Pop said. 'You couldn't wish for nothing more perfick nowhere.'

2

WHEN Mariette and Mr Charlton came down from the bluebell wood an hour later, Mariette carrying a bunch of bluebells and pink campion, Mr Charlton bearing in his palm, with
the tenderest care, two blue thrushes' eggs a bird had dropped
in the grass at the woodside, Pop was washing pig-buckets
under the tap in the yard.

'Pigs look well,' Pop said. 'I think we'll kill one. Hear the
nightingales?'

Mr Charlton had not a second in which to answer this
question before Pop said:

'Wondering where you two had got to, Mister Charlton.
Tea's ready. Just in time.'

A searching odour of frying kippers cut almost savagely
through the warm May air.

'I thought we just had tea,' Mr Charlton said.

'That was dinner.'

'I ought to catch my bus,' Mr Charlton said. 'I must. The
last one goes at eight o'clock.'

'Ma won't hear of that,' Pop said. 'Will she, Mariette?
Daresay Mariette won't either. Like to wash your hands?
What you got there?'

Mr Charlton revealed the thrushes' eggs, brilliant blue in his
office-pale hands, and Mariette gave him a small dark smile of
fascination that held him once more transfixed and speechless.

'Always run you home in the truck,' Pop said. 'Next time
you come out you must bring your car. What kind of car you
got, Mister Charlton?'

Mr Charlton confessed that he had no car. Pop was stunned.

'No car, no car?' he said. 'That'll never do. Can't have that. Hear that, Mariette? Mister Charlton ain't got no car.'

'I don't think I'll have the time to come out again,' Mr Charlton said. 'Do you think we could go into the question of the tax form before I go? It's very important.'

'Tea first,' Pop said. 'Must have a cuppa tea first. Don't want to make Ma mad, do you?'

Pop finished drying his hands and gave Mr Charlton the towel. Mr Charlton put the two thrushes' eggs into his pocket and ran tap water over his hands, washing them with a gritty cake of purple soap. Mariette gave him another intimate, flashing smile and then went towards the house, calling that she was going to powder her nose, and Mr Charlton, completely captivated by the delicate vision of green shantung retreating in the golden evening sunshine, forgot the thrushes' eggs and said:

'I don't know if you appreciate how severe the penalties are for not making a tax return, Mr Larkin.'

'Ma's calling,' Pop said.

Mr Charlton listened but couldn't hear a sound.

'I shall have to make some sort of report to my office,' Mr Charlton said. 'Then if you don't cooperate it'll be taken out of my hands and after that –'

'Beautiful evening, ain't it?' Pop said. Once again, caught in his own web of enchantment, he turned to stare at an evening distilled now into even deeper gold by the lower angle of light falling across still seas of buttercups and long-curled milky waves of may.

'I strongly recommend you –'

'Pair o' goldfinches,' Pop said, but Mr Charlton was too slow to see the birds, which darted past him like dipping sparks of scarlet, black, and gold.

In the kitchen Ma was frying a third batch of four fat tawny kippers in a brand new aluminium pan while Mariette powdered her face over the sink, looking into a heart-shaped mirror stuck about with little silver, pink, and violet seashells.

'How'd you get on with Mr Charlton, duckie?'

'Slow,' Mariette said. 'He's very shy.'

'Well, he mustn't be shy,' Ma said. 'That won't get you nowhere.'

'He would talk about horses.'

'You'll have to find something a bit better than that to talk about, won't you?' Ma said. 'Bit more stimulating.'

Mariette, who was busy making up her lips with a tender shade of pink, not at all unlike the pink of the rose campion, that went well with her dress of cool lime shantung, did not answer.

'I think he looks half-starved,' Ma said. 'No blood in him. Wants feeding up. I'll find him a good fat kipper.'

Mariette was wetting small wisps of short hair with her finger-tips and winding them about her ears like black watch-springs.

'Put some of my Goya on,' Ma said. 'The gardenia. Or else the Chanel. They both stand by my jewel-box in our bedroom.'

While Mariette went upstairs to dab perfume behind her ears and in soft hollows of her legs, Mr Charlton and Pop came in from the yard to join Montgomery, Primrose, Victoria, and the twins, who sat at the table licking thick bars of choc-ice and watching a television programme in which three men, a clergyman, and a woman were discussing prostitution and what should be done about it all.

'Strawberry-picking on Monday over at Benacre, Pop,' Montgomery said. 'I heard from Fred Brown.'

'That's early,' Pop said. 'Earliest we've ever been. I said this wevver'd soon put the paint on 'em.'

Ma came in bearing a big dish of stinging hot kippers running with fat dabs of butter and on the television screen the woman shook a condemnatory finger at the gaping children and said: 'The women are, on the whole, less to be blamed than pitied. It is largely the fault of man.'

'Ma,' Pop said. 'Strawberry-picking Monday. Better get that deep-freeze, hadn't we?'

'Sooner the better,' Ma said. 'Better go in first thing tomorrow. It's Saturday.' She began to serve kippers. 'Start pouring tea, Primrose. Kipper, Mister Charlton? Here we come. Nice fat one. Help yourself to more butter if you want to.'

While Ma served kippers and Primrose poured tea Pop rose from the table and fetched a bottle of whisky from the cocktail cabinet.

'Milk?' he said to Ma.

'Please,' Ma said. 'Just what I need.'

Pop poured whisky into Ma's tea, then into his own, and then turned to Mr Charlton, the bottle upraised.

'Drop o' milk, Mister Charlton?'

'No, no, no. No really. Not for me. No really not for me.'

'Relieves the wind, frees the kidneys, and opens the bowels,' Pop said blandly.

'No, no. No really. Not at this time of day.'

'Do you all the good in the world, Mister Charlton.'

Pop, after filling up Mr Charlton's tea-cup with whisky, stood for a moment staring at the television screen and said:

'What the ruddy 'ell are they talking about? Kids, how much money you make on the stall?'

'Eighteenpence. There was a policeman on a motor-bike come along.'

'Pity he hadn't got summat else to do,' Pop said.

With elbows on the table Victoria, who was trying to eat kipper with a spoon, said in a shrill quick voice:

'I don't like kippers. They're made of combs.'

'Now, now,' Pop said. 'Now, now. Manners, manners. Elbows!'

'Pop has 'em at a word,' Ma said.

Mr Charlton sat held in a new constriction of bewilderment made more complex by the arrival of Mariette, fresh and lovely with new pink lipstick, face powder, and a heavy fragrance of gardenias that overwhelmed him in a cloud of intoxication as she came and sat at his side.

As if this were not enough she had brought with her the bluebells and the rose campion, arranged in an orange and crimson jar. She set the jar in the centre of the table, where the flowers glowed in the nightmare marine glow of the television light like a strange sheaf of sea-weed. The bluebells too smelt exquisitely.

'Sorry I'm late,' she whispered to Mr Charlton and he could have sworn, in another moment of shimmering agony, that her silky legs had brushed his own. 'Just had to make myself presentable.'

'By the way, Mister Charlton,' Pop said, 'what's your other name? Don't like this mistering.'

'Cedric.'

Ma started choking.

'Kipper bone!' Pop said. 'Happened once before.'

He rose from the table and struck Ma a severe blow in the middle of the back. She boomed like a drum.

'Better?' Pop said and hit her a second time, rather more robustly than the first.

Except for bouncing slightly Ma did not seem to mind at all.

'Worst of kippers,' Pop said. 'Too much wire-work. Fetched it up?'

On the television screen a man in close-up stared with steadfast earnestness at Mr Charlton and the eight Larkins and said: 'Well, there it is. We leave it with you. What do you think? What is to be done about these women? Is it their fault? Is it the fault of men? If not, whose fault is it?' and once again, for the third time, Ma started laughing like a jelly.

'Play crib at all, Mister Charlton?' Pop said.

Mr Charlton had to confess he had never heard of crib.

'Card game,' Pop said. 'We all play here. Learns you figures. Mariette plays. Mariette could show you how.'

Mr Charlton turned to look shyly at Mariette and found his vision, already blurred by the curious light from the television screen, clouded into more numbing and exquisite confusion by the thick sweet fragrance of gardenia. In return she gazed at him with dark silent eyes, so that he could not help trembling and was even glad when Pop said:

'Like billiards? Or snooker? Got a nice table out the back there. Full size. We could have a game o' snooker after tea.'

'You know,' Mr Charlton said, 'I'm really awfully sorry, but I must catch this eight o'clock bus.'

'No eight o'clock bus now,' Montgomery said. 'They knocked it off soon after petrol rationing started.'

'That's right,' Ma said. 'They never put it back again.'

Mr Charlton half-rose from the table, agitated.

'In that case I must start walking. It's eight miles.'

'Walking my foot,' Pop said. 'I said I'll run you home in the truck. Or else Mariette can take you in the station-wagon. Mariette can drive. Mariette'll take you, won't you, Mariette?'

'Of course.'

Mr Charlton sat down, mesmerized.

'Why don't you stay the night?' Pop said. 'That's all right, ain't it, Ma?'

'More the merrier.'

'Perfick,' Pop said. 'Ma'll make you a bed up on the billiard table.'

'No, really –'

'It's so simple,' Mariette said. 'After all tomorrow's Saturday. You don't have to go to the office Saturday, do you?'

'Course he don't,' Pop said. 'Offices don't work Saturdays. They don't none of 'em know what work is no more.'

'That's settled then,' Ma said. 'I'll put him on that new super-foam mattress Mariette has for sun-bathing.'

'Oh! that mattress is marvellous,' Mariette said. 'You sink in. Your body simply dreams into that mattress.'

In another unnerving moment Mr Charlton saw the girl, hands raised to her bare shoulders, luxuriously enact for him the attitudes of dreaming into the mattress. As her eyes closed and her lips parted gently he struggled to bring himself back to reality, firmness, and a state of resistance and he said:

'No, I'm sorry. I really must be adamant –'

Pop stared with open mouth, powerfully stunned and impressed by this word. He could not ever remember having heard it even on television.

'Quite understand,' he said.

In a single moment Mr Charlton was raised greatly in his estimation. He looked at him with awe.

'Oh! won't you stay?' Mariette said. 'We could ride to-morrow.'

Groping again, struggling against the dark eyes and the fragrance of gardenia, powerful even above the penetrating sting of kippers, Mr Charlton began to say:

'No, really. For one thing I've nothing with me. I've no pyjamas.'

'Gawd Almighty,' Pop said. 'Pyjamas?'

His admiration and awe for Mr Charlton now increased still further. He was held transfixed by the fact that here was a man who spoke in words of inaccessible meaning and wore pyjamas to sleep in.

'Sleep in your shirt, old man,' he said. 'Like I do.'

Pop had always slept in his shirt; he found it more convenient that way. Ma, on the other hand, slept in nylon nightgowns, one of them an unusual pale petunia-pink that Pop liked more than all the rest because it was light, delicate, and above all completely transparent. It was wonderful for seeing through. Under it Ma's body appeared like a global map, an expanse of huge explorable mountains, shadowy valleys, and rosy pinnacles.

'I wear pyjamas,' Mariette said. 'I'll lend you a pair of mine.'

'No, really –'

Mr Charlton became utterly speechless as Ma got up, went into the kitchen and brought back four tins of whole peaches, which she began to open with an elaborate tin-opener on the sideboard.

'Save some of the juice, Ma,' Pop said. 'I'll have it later with a drop o' gin.'

'I think you're about my size,' Mariette said, as if every-thing were now completely settled, so that Mr Charlton found himself in the centre of a shattering vortex, trapped there by the torturing and incredible thought that presently he would be sleeping in Mariette's own pyjamas, on her own dreaming bed of foam.

Before he could make any further protest about this Prim-rose poured him a second cup of tea and Pop, leaning across the table, filled it up with whisky.

'You ought to come strawberry-picking,' Pop said. Mr Charlton suddenly remembered the tax form. It mustn't be forgotten, he thought, the tax form. On no account must it be forgotten. 'This is very like the last summer we'll ever go strawberry-picking, Mister Charlton. We, you, anybody. You know why?'

Tax form, tax form, tax form, Mr Charlton kept thinking. Tax form. 'No. Why?'

On the television screen a voice announced: 'We now take you to Fanshawe Castle, the home of the Duke of Peele,' and Ma, ladling out the last of the peaches, crowned by thick ovals of cream, said:

'Turn up the contrast. I want to see this. It's got dark again.'

'Because', Pop said, 'the strawberry lark's nearly over.'

Tax form, tax form, tax form, Mr Charlton thought again. How was it the strawberry lark was nearly over? Tax form.

'Disease,' Pop said. 'Sovereigns are finished. Climax is finished. Huxleys are finished. Soon there won't be no straw-berries nowhere.'

Tax form. 'You mean that in this great strawberry-growing district –'

'This districk. Every districk. In two years the strawberry lark'll be over.'

38

'Well, myself, I actually prefer raspberries –'

'The raspberry lark's nearly over as well,' Pop said. 'Mosaic. Weakening strain. And the plum lark. And the cherry lark. And the apple lark. They can't sell apples for love nor –'

'We're in the library,' Ma said. 'Pop, look at the library.'

Tax form – Mr Charlton, with piteous desperation, struggled with the power of all his declining concentration to see that the tax form was remembered. 'I've got to go home,' he thought. 'I've got to start walking.' Something brushed his leg. 'I must remember the tax form.' He was startled into a sudden shivering catch of his breath and a moment later the white kitten was on his knee.

'Gawd Almighty,' Pop said. 'What are all them on the walls?'

'Must be books,' Ma said.

In mute staring concentration Pop sat involved by the picture on the television screen, noisily eating peaches and taking an occasional quick-sucked gulp of whisky and tea.

'Never,' he said. 'Can't be.'

'Beautiful home,' Ma said. 'I like the pelmets. That's what we want. Pelmets like that.'

Tax form! Mr Charlton's mind shouted. Tax form –!

'Books?' Pop said. '*All* books?'

'I'll go and find the pyjamas and get them aired,' Mariette said. Mr Charlton emerged from a moment of acute hypnosis to feel her hand reach out, touch him softly, and then begin to draw him away. 'Coming? We could try them against you for size.'

'The man who owns that owes five million tax,' Mr Charlton said desperately and for no reason at all. 'Mr Larkin, that reminds me – we mustn't forget that form –'

'Perfick place,' Pop said. 'On the big side though. Suppose they need it for the books.'

'Oh! the carpets. Look at the carpets,' Ma said. 'There must be miles of carpets. Acres.'

'He'll have to give it all up,' Mr Charlton said. 'The State will take it for taxes. You see what can happen –'

'Come on,' Mariette said and Mr Charlton, struggling for the last time against the flickering, rising tides of sea-green light rolling across the table in mesmeric, engulfing flow, followed the girl blunderingly into the kitchen, the white kitten softly brushing his legs as he went, the thick night-sweet scent of gardenia penetrating to his blood, seeming to turn it as white as the flower from which it sprang.

3

A T half past ten, just before television closed down for the night, Pop, Ma, and Mariette were still trying to teach Mr Charlton the mysteries and arithmetic of crib. Utterly baffled – the only coherent thing he had been able to do all evening was to telephone his landlady to say that he wouldn't be coming home that night – Mr Charlton found it quite impossible to understand the elements of the game, still less its language and figures.

'Fifteen-two, fifteen-four, fifteen-six, pair's eight, three's eleven, three's fourteen, and one for his nob's fifteen.'

Pop dealt the cards very fluidly; he counted like a machine.

'I don't understand one for his nob.'

'Jack,' Pop said. 'I told you – one for his nob. Two for his heels. Your deal, Ma.'

Ma dealt very fluidly too.

'Got to use your loaf at this game, Mister Charlton,' Pop said. 'I thought you was office man? I thought you was good at figures?'

'Rather different sort of figures,' Mr Charlton said.

'Oh?' Pop said. 'Really? They look all the same to me.'

Pop picked up the cards Ma had dealt him, took a quick look at them, and said smartly:

'Mis-deal. Seven cards. Bung in.'

'Pick 'em up!' Ma said and threatened him with a hand as large as a leg of lamb. 'Don't you dare.'

'Wanted a Parson's Poke,' Pop said.

'No more Parson's Pokes,' Ma said. 'Get on with it. Make

the best with what you've got.' Ma kicked Mr Charlton playfully on the shins under the table, laughing. 'Got to watch him, Mister Charlton, playing crib. Parson's Poke, my foot. Sharp as a packet o' pins.'

'Twenty-two, nine'll do. Twenty-five, six's is alive. Twenty-eight, Billy Wake. Twenty-seven, four's in heaven. Twenty-three, eight's a spree.'

In the combined turmoil of counting and the glare of the television Mr Charlton felt a certain madness coming back.

'What you got, Pop?'

'Terrible. What Paddy shot at.'

'See what I mean?' Ma said. She kicked Mr Charlton a second time on the shins, just as playfully as the first. 'Mis-deal my foot! No wonder he says you got to use your loaf at this game. Your deal next, Mr Charlton. Your box.'

Mr Charlton, as he picked up the cards, was beginning to feel that he had no loaf to use. He felt awful; his loaf was like a sponge.

'Let's have a Parson's Poke!' Pop said.

'No more Parson's Pokes,' Ma said. 'Too many Parson's Pokes are bad luck.'

'Your box, Mr Charlton. Give yourself a treat.'

'Let him play his own game!' Ma said. 'Play your own hand, Mr Charlton. Use your own loaf. What's on telly now?'

'Something about free speech,' Mariette said. 'Freedom of the press or something.'

Pop turned his head, looking casually at the flickering screen. On it four heated men were, it seemed, about to start fighting.

'Wherever conditions of uniform tolerance may be said to obtain –'

'Barmy,' Ma said. 'Want their heads testing.'

'The trouble with telly,' Pop said, 'it don't go on long enough.'

'You miss it when you're talking,' Ma said. 'You feel lost, somehow. Don't you think you feel lost, Mr Charlton?'

Mr Charlton had to confess he felt lost.

'I like this set better than the other,' Ma said. 'Better contrast.'

'Thirsty, Ma?' Pop said. 'I'm thirsty.'

During the evening Pop had drunk the remainder of the peach-juice, laced with gin, two bottles of Guinness, and a light ale. Mr Charlton had drunk two glasses of beer. Ma and Mariette had been drinking cider.

'I'll mix a cocktail,' Pop said. 'Mister Charlton, what about a cocktail?'

'You don't want no more,' Ma said. 'You'll want to get out in the night.'

'I'm thirsty,' Pop said. 'I'm parched up.'

'You'll be pickled.'

Pop was already on his feet, moving towards the expensive glass and chromium cocktail cabinet that stood in one corner. 'Sit down and play your hand.'

Pop stood by the cabinet, his pride hurt and offended.

'Never been pickled in me life,' he said. 'Anyway not more than once or twice a week. And then only standin'-up pickled.'

Was there some difference between that and other forms? Mr Charlton wondered.

'Layin'-down pickled,' Pop said, 'of course.'

'I'm getting tired of crib,' Mariette said. 'It's hot in here. I'm going to cool off in the yard, Mr Charlton.' Like her father she found it difficult to call Mr Charlton by his Christian name. 'Like to come?'

'After he's had a cocktail,' Pop said. 'I'm going to mix everybody a special cocktail.'

While Mariette packed up the cards, the pegs, and the pegboard Pop stood by the cocktail cabinet consulting a book, *A Guide to Better Drinking*, given him by Montgomery for Christmas. It was the only book he had ever read.

'Here's one we never tried,' Pop said. 'Rolls-Royce.'

'That sounds nice,' Ma said.

'Half vermouth, quarter whisky, quarter gin, dash of orange bitters.'

'Dash you will too,' Ma said, 'with that lot. It'll blow our heads off.'

'Blow summat off,' Pop said. 'Not sure what though.'

Once again Ma started laughing like a jelly.

'How do you like our cocktail cabinet, Mister Charlton?' Pop said. 'Only had it at Christmas. Cost us a hundred and fifty.'

'Hundred and eighty,' Ma said. 'We had that other model in the end. The one with the extra sets of goblets. The brandy lot. You remember. And the silver bits for hot punch and all that.'

With confusion and awe Mr Charlton stared at the cocktail cabinet, over which Pop hovered, mixing the drinks, in his shirt sleeves. The cabinet, he realized for the first time, seemed shaped like an elaborate glass and silver ship.

'Am I mistaken?' he said. 'Or is it a ship?'

'Spanish galleon,' Pop said. 'Heigh-ho and a bottle o' rum and all that lark.'

When the cocktail was mixed Pop poured it into four large cut-glass tumblers embellished with scarlet cockerels. He had mixed it double, he said. It saved a lot of time like that.

'Try it first,' Ma said. 'We don't want it if it's no good, Rolls-Royce or no Rolls-Royce. Besides, you might fall down dead.'

Pop drained the shaker.

'Perfick,' he said. 'This'll grow hair.'

'By the way,' Ma said, 'talking about Rolls-Royce, did you do anything about that one?'

'Sunday,' Pop said. 'The chap's a stock-broker. Colonel Forbes. He's only down week-ends.'

'Pop's mad on a Rolls,' Ma explained to Mr Charlton.

'By the way, Mister Charlton,' Pop said, 'what was that about that feller on telly owing five million tax? Was that right?'

'Perfectly correct.'

'What for?'

'Death duties.'

'Deaf duties!' Pop said. 'Deaf duties! I feel like murder every time I hear deaf duties!'

Pop, snorting with disgust and irritation, struck the table with the palm of his hand and as if by a pre-arranged signal the light in the television went out. Ma uttered a sudden cry as if something terrible had happened. Mariette got up suddenly and switched the set off and there floated by Mr Charlton's face, as she passed, a fresh wave of gardenia, warm as the evening itself, disturbed and disturbing as she moved.

'That made my head jump,' Ma said. 'I thought a valve had gone.'

'Closing down, that's all,' Pop said. 'Eleven o'clock and they're closing down. Hardly got started.'

Pop, giving another snort of disgust about death duties and the brief and contemptible daily compass of television, handed round the cocktails.

'Cheers, everybody,' he said, raising glass. 'Here's to the strawberry lark. Roll on Monday.'

Mr Charlton drank. A wave of pure alcohol burned the roots off his tongue. He was utterly unable to speak for some moments and could only listen with undivided and searing agony to a question, first from Pop and then from Mariette, about whether he could be with them on Monday for the strawberry lark.

'I – I – I –'

A sensation as of a white-hot stiletto descending rapidly towards Mr Charlton's navel prevented the sentence from developing beyond a single choking word.

'Make yourself fifteen or twenty quid in no time,' Pop said. 'All the strawberries you can eat. And a pound free every day. You can gather a hundred and fifty pounds a day.'

'I – I – I –'

Burning tears came into Mr Charlton's eyes. He succeeded in murmuring at last, with a tongue cauterized of all feeling and in a voice that did not belong to him, something about work, office, and having no leave.

'You could always come in the evenings,' Mariette said. 'Plenty of people do.'

As she said this she again turned and looked at him. The eyes seemed more tenderly, intensely, darkly penetrative than ever and he began flushing deeply.

'It's lovely in the evenings,' Mariette said. 'Absolutely lovely.'

Another draught of alcohol, snatched by Mr Charlton in another desperate moment of speechlessness, injected fire into remote interior corners of his body that he did not know existed.

'My God, this is a perfick pick-me-up,' Pop said. 'We must all have another one of those.'

Mr Charlton despaired and passed a groping hand over his face. His mouth burned, as from eating ginger. He heard Ma agree that the cocktail was a beauty. He actually heard her say that they owed everybody in the neighbourhood a drink. 'What say we have a cocktail party and give them this one? This'll get under their skin.'

That, Mr Charlton heard himself saying, was what was happening to him, but nobody seemed to hear a voice that was already inexplicably far away, except that Ma once again began laughing, piercingly, the salmon jumper shaking like a vast balloon.

'A few more of these and you won't see me for dust,' she said.

'A few more?' Mr Charlton heard himself saying. 'A few more?'

'First re-fill coming up, Mister Charlton. How do you like it? Ma, I bet this would go well with a bloater-paste sandwich.'

Something about this remark made Mr Charlton start laughing too. This enlivening development was a signal for Pop to strike Mr Charlton a severe blow in the back, exactly as he had done Ma, and call him a rattlin' good feller. 'Feel you're one of the family. Feel we've known you years. That right, Ma?'

That was right, Ma said. That was the truth. That was how they felt about him.

'Honest trufe,' Pop said. 'Honest trufe, Mister Charlton.'

A wave of unsteady pleasure, like a flutter of ruffling wind across water on a summer afternoon, ran through Mr Charlton's veins and set them dancing. He drank again. He felt a sudden lively and uncontrollable desire to pick strawberries on warm midsummer evenings, no matter what happened. 'My

God, this is great stuff,' he told everybody. 'This is the true essence –'

Nobody knew what Mr Charlton was talking about. It was impossible to grasp what he meant by the true essence, but it set Ma laughing again. Somewhere behind the laughter Mr Charlton heard Pop mixing a third, perhaps a fourth, re-fill, saying at the same time 'Only thing it wants is more ice. More ice, Ma!'

Mr Charlton, for no predetermined reason, suddenly rose and struck himself manfully on the chest.

'I'll get it,' he said. 'That's me. I'm the ice-man.'

When Mr Charlton came back from the kitchen, carrying trays of ice, Pop mixed the new drink and tasted it with slow, appraising tongue and eye.

'More perfick than ever!'

Everything was more perfick, Mr Charlton kept telling himself. The scent of gardenia was more perfick. It too was stronger than ever. He laughed immoderately, for no reason, and at length, looking for the first time straight into the dark searching eyes of Mariette with neither caution nor despair.

'Mariette,' he said, 'what is the scent you're wearing?'

'Come and sit over here and I'll tell you.'

Mr Charlton moved to sit on the other side of the table. Rising abruptly, he stood stunned. It seemed to him that something remarkable had happened to Pop. Pop, it seemed to him, had disappeared.

'I didn't see Pop go out,' he said. 'Where's Pop gone?'

Ma began shrieking.

'I'm under here!' Pop said.

'Under me! I'm sitting on his lap,' Ma said. 'Why don't you ask Mariette if she'll sit on yours?'

Mariette, who needed no asking, sat on Mr Charlton's lap.

The illusion of being caressed in a silken, sinuous, maddening way by the goose's neck returned to Mr Charlton as he felt her silken legs cross his own. A sensation that for the second time his blood was turning white, while being at the same time on fire, coursed completely through him. The soles of his feet started tingling. The scent of gardenia overwhelmed him like a drug.

'Tell me what the scent is,' Mr Charlton said.

'Gardenia.'

'Gardenia? Gardenia? What's gardenia?'

'It's a flower. Do you like it?'

'Like it? Like it?' Mr Charlton said madly. 'Like it?'

With extraordinarily soft hands Mariette took his own and held them high round her waist, just under her breasts. With stupefying tenderness she started to rock backwards and forwards on his knee, with the result that Mr Charlton could not see straight. His eyes were simply two quivering balls revolving unrestrainedly in the top of his head.

'Well, getting late,' Pop said. 'Hitch up a bit, Ma, and I'll mix another before we go to shut-eye.'

Pop reappeared presently from underneath the salmon canopy of Ma and announced that he was going to mix a new one this time.

'How about a Chauffeur? Dammit, the Rolls has to have a Chauffeur,' he said. He stood earnestly consulting the *Guide to Better Drinking*. 'One third vermouth, one third whisky, one third gin, dash of angostura. Sounds perfick. Everybody game?'

Everybody was game. Mr Charlton was very game. He said so over and over again. Mariette held his hands more closely against her body and a little higher than before and Mr Charlton let his head rest against the velvety, downy nape of her dark neck.

'You're my goose. My gardenia,' he said.

'Wouldn't you think', Mariette said, 'that it was soon time to go to bed?'

Some moments later Mr Charlton had drained the Chauffeur in two gulps and was addressing Ma and Pop in what he thought were solid, steadfast tones of gratitude.

'Can never thank you. Never thank you. Never be able to thank you.'

He shook on his feet, grasped at air with aimless hands, and started jiggling like a fish.

'Should be a cocktail called gardenia! A sweet one –'

'I'll make one,' Pop said. 'I'll think one up.'

'And one called Mariette,' Mr Charlton said. 'Sweet one too! –'

He staggered violently and some time later was vaguely aware of walking arm in arm to the billiard-room with Mariette. There was no light in the billiard-room. He felt filled with inconsolable happiness and laughed with wild immoderation, once again feeling her legs brush against him like the goose-neck, in the darkness. Once again too he called her a gardenia and stretched out groping hands to touch her.

Instead, unsurprised, he found himself kneeling by the billiard table, caressing in the corner pocket a solitary, cool abandoned ball.

'Where are you? Where are you?' he said. 'Mariette –'

Mr Charlton got up and fell down, breaking the thrushes' eggs in his pocket as he fell.

'Climb up,' Mariette said. Mr Charlton found it impossible to climb up and Mariette started pushing him. 'Upsadaisy. Up you go. I'll get your collar off.'

Meanwhile Pop, who was sitting up in bed in his shirt, thinking of the evening sunshine, the meadows shining so beautifully and so golden with buttercups and the prospect of summer growing to maturity all about his paradise, decided that the only thing to make the day more perfick was a cigar.

'I'm the same as Churchill,' he said. 'Like a good cigar.'

He lit the cigar and sat watching Ma undress herself. The thing he really loved most about Ma, he had long since decided, was that she didn't have to wear corsets. She didn't need them; her figure was all her own; pure and natural as could be.

'Ma, I've been thinking,' he said, 'when does Mariette expect this baby?'

'She can't make up her mind.'

'Well, she'd better,' Pop said.

'Why?' Ma said.

From the depths of her transparent petunia canopy, as it floated down over the global map of her white, wide territory, Ma spoke with her customary air of unconcern.

Smoking his cigar, gazing thoughtfully through the open window to a night of warm May stars, as if pondering again on summer and the way it would soon embroider with its gold and green his already perfick paradise, Pop made a pronouncement.

'I'm a bit worried about Mister Charlton. I don't think that young man's got it in 'im,' he said. 'At least not yet.'

4

MR CHARLTON woke late and to a dark, disquieting impression. It was that he was lying alone in the centre of a large flat green field. A cold storm was raging about him. Overhead drummed peals of thunder.

Agony taught him some minutes later that the thunder rolled from somewhere inside his own head and that the field was the billiard table, from which he was about to fall. He got up off the table and groped with uncertain agony about the semi-darkened room, white hands limp at his sides, stringy and strengthless, like portions of tired celery.

He was wearing Mariette's pyjamas, which were silk, of a pale blue colour, with a pattern of either pink roses or carnations all over them – he was too distraught to tell which. He could not remember putting the pyjamas on. He could only suppose Mariette had put them on. He could not remember that either.

Presently, after managing to pull on his trousers over his pyjamas, he groped his way out of the billiard-room. In the kitchen the apparition of Ma, now wearing a parma-violet jumper instead of the salmon one, overrode all other objects, like a circus elephant. She was making toast and frying eggs and bacon. His hands trembled as they grasped a chair.

'Ah! there you are, Mister Charlton. One egg or two?' Ma, in her customary fashion, started laughing like a jelly, her voice a carillon. 'Two eggs or three? Sleep all right?'

Mr Charlton sat down and thought that even if wild dogs had begun to chase him he would never again have the strength to move.

'Cuppa tea?' A heavy weight, like a descending pile-driver, hit the table, shaking cups and cutlery. It was a cup. 'Like a drop of milk in it?' With shaking bosom Ma roared happily again. 'Cows or Johnny Walker?'

Mr Charlton prayed silently over the comforting fumes of tea.

'Mariette waited for you but you didn't seem to come so she's gone for a ride now to get her appetite up,' Ma said. 'She'll be back any minute now. Pop's feeding the pigs. He's had one breakfast. But he'll want another.'

Life, Mr Charlton felt, was ebbing away from him. In his cup large tea-leaves swam dizzily round and round, the black wreckage of disaster.

'You never said how many eggs,' Ma said. 'One or two? How do you like 'em? Turned over?'

'I –'

A moment later a rough sledge-hammer hit Mr Charlton in the middle of the back.

'How's the tax-man?' Pop said. 'How's my friend? All right, old man? Sleep well? Perfick morning, ain't it?'

Whereas overnight Mr Charlton's veins had run white, in crazy, voluptuous courses, he now felt them to be some shade of pale, expiring green. There was also something seriously wrong with his intestines. They were dissolving under waves of acid. He could no longer claim them for his own.

'I don't think Mr Charlton feels very well,' Ma said.

'No?' Pop said. 'Pity. Didn't sleep very well? Potted the white, eh?' Pop barked with violent laughter at his joke. 'Hair of the dog I should say.'

Mr Charlton had never heard of hair of the dog. Pop sat down at the table and drummed on it with the handles of his knife and fork, whistling *Come to the cook-house door, boys* through his teeth.

'What's your programme this morning, old man? Like to come with me and take the pig over to the bacon factory?'

'I think I shall have to go home.'

Faintly Mr Charlton spoke for the first time, his voice full of pallid distress. Echoes of his words rang through his head in hollow tones, as through a sepulchre.

'Don't say that, old man,' Pop said. 'We was looking forward to having you the whole week-end. I want to show you the place. I got thirty-two acres here altogether. Lovely big medder at the back. Beautiful stretch o' river. Perfick. Do any fishing?'

While Pop was speaking Ma set before him a plate of three eggs, four six-inch rashers of home-cured bacon, three very thick brown sausages, and a slice of fried bread. Pop attacked this with the precipitate virility and desperation of a man who has not seen food for some long time. In an excruciating moment the last of Mr Charlton's intestines got ready to dissolve.

Suddenly Pop slapped down his knife and fork, troubled.

'Something wrong?' Ma said.

'Don't taste right.'

'You forgot the ketchup, you loony, that's why.'

'Gorblimey, so I did. Knowed there was summat wrong somewhere.'

Pop reached out, grabbed the ketchup bottle, and shook an ocean of scarlet all over his breakfast.

Mr Charlton shut his eyes. This grave mistake made him think that he was on the deck of a sinking ship, in a hurricane. He opened his eyes with great haste and the deck came up at him.

'Hullo there, bright eyes. Good morning. How are we this morning?'

The astral figure of Mariette, fresh in yellow shirt and jodhpurs, was all that Mr Charlton felt he needed to set him weeping. The pristine, cheerful voice was beyond his range of thought. He tried to say something and failed, faintly.

'Mister Charlton doesn't feel all that well,' Ma said. 'He says he might have to go home.'

Pop belched with enormous pleasure, as usual surprising himself.

'Manners. Early morning breeze. Pardon me.' He struck his chest with the handle of the fork, as if in stern reproval. 'Home, my foot. Stop worrying, old man. That's the trouble with you office fellers. You all worry too much by half. After all, here today and gone tomorrow.'

It was not tomorrow, Mr Charlton thought, that he was worried about. Unless he could find some speedy, drastic remedy he would, he was convinced, be gone today.

'Heavens, I'm hungry,' Mariette said.

She sat down at the table, stirred a cup of tea, and started laughing. Her voice put stitches into Mr Charlton's head: stabbing lines of them, on hot needles.

'See something funny out riding?' Pop said. 'Like the Brigadier's sister?'

'I was just smiling at Mr Charlton. He's still got the pyjamas on.' She started laughing again and Mr Charlton could not help feeling there was some sinister, hidden meaning in the word smiling. 'Oh! that was a laugh, getting them on last night. First we couldn't get one lot of trousers off and then we couldn't get the other lot on. Oh! Mr Charlton, you were a scream. Absolute scream.'

Mr Charlton, who began to feel among other things that he was not grown up, did not doubt it. Everything was a scream. His whole body, his entire mind, and his intestines were a scream.

'Most of the time you were making love to a billiard ball in the side pocket.'

Pop started choking.

'I said you potted the white, didn't I?' he shouted. 'Ain't that what I said, Ma?' With immense glee Pop beat a tattoo on the table-cloth with the handles of his knife and fork. 'Potted the white. Damn funny. Just what I said.'

'Tonight I'll make you a proper bed up,' Ma said. 'In the bottom bathroom. Nobody uses it very much now we've got the new one upstairs.'

'I really think', Mr Charlton said, his voice limp, 'I'd better go home.'

In a sudden gesture of fond solicitude Pop put an arm round Mr Charlton's shoulder.

'You know, Charley boy,' he said, 'I wish your name was Charley instead of Cedric. It's more human. I can't get used to Cedric. It's like a parson's name. Can't we call you Charley? – after all it's short for your other name.'

'Please call me Charley if you wish,' Mr Charlton said and felt once again like weeping.

'What I was going to say, Charley boy,' Pop went on, 'is this, old man, I think you need a Larkin Special.'

Mr Charlton had no time to ask what a Larkin Special was before Pop was out of the room, across the passage, and into the living-room on the other side. Presently there were noises from the Spanish galleon, the monster cocktail cabinet that could have only been moulded, Mr Charlton thought, by a man of evil, demoniac designs.

'That'll put you as right as a lamplighter in no time,' Ma said. 'Acts like a charm.'

'A nice walk after breakfast,' Mariette said, 'and you'll be on top of the world.' Mr Charlton felt sure that that in fact was where he was, but in the act of falling. Mariette was now eating bacon, eggs, large burnished brown sausages, and fried bread. 'We could walk across the meadow and have a look at the motor-boat if you like.'

'Motor-boat?' At the same moment some curious reflex of thought made Mr Charlton remember the buff-yellow tax form. He hadn't seen it since sharing his boiled eggs with the twins the previous day. 'You've got a motor-boat?'

'Nice one. Little beauty. We keep it in the boathouse on the other side of the meadow.'

'Pop took it in exchange for a debt,' Ma explained.

'Mrs Larkin,' Mr Charlton began to say. He felt suddenly, in a guilty fashion, that he ought to make some sort of atonement with himself for all that had happened. He was actually bothered by a sense of duty. 'I don't suppose you've seen that buff-yellow form –'

'Coming up, coming up, coming up,' Pop said. 'There you are, Charley, old man. Larkin Special. Don't ask what's in it. Don't stare at it. Don't think. Just drink it down. In ten minutes you'll feel perfick again.'

Pop set before a demoralized Mr Charlton, on the breakfast table, what Mr Charlton could only think was a draught of bull's blood.

'I think I should go and lie down –'

'Don't think a thing!' Pop said. 'Drink it. Say to 'ell wiv everything and drink it.'

Mr Charlton hesitated. His intestines rolled.

'I can vouch for it,' Ma said.

The soft dark eyes of Mariette smiled across the table. The familiar astral vision of cool olive skin against the light lemon shirt, of dark hair and the firm treasured breasts that Mr Charlton had almost clasped the previous evening, revived an inspiring, momentary recollection of his lost white fire.

He ducked his head and drank.

'Now I must get cracking,' Pop said. 'I got a bit of a deal to do about some straw. I got the new deep-freeze to pick up. And the pigs. And the port.'

With fond assurance he laid a hand on Mr Charlton's shoulder.

'Charley, old man,' he said, 'by the time I get back you'll feel perfick.'

For some time Mr Charlton sat in tentative silence, re-awaking. A feeling of slow intestinal restoration made him give, once or twice, a tender sigh. He grasped slowly that the thunder in his head had now become mere singing, like distant vespers in a minor key.

'Feeling more yourself now?'

Mariette was eating toast and golden marmalade. As she opened her mouth to eat he saw, for the first time, how beautifully white her teeth were and how pink, in a pure rose-petal shade, her tongue now appeared as it darted out and caught at golden shreds of marmalade.

He even found himself thinking of gardenia, its compelling, torturing night-scent and the pure whiteness of its flower.

'It's absolutely wonderful in the woods this morning,' Mariette said. 'All the bluebells out. Millions of them. And the moon-daisies. It's hot too and the nightingales had already started when I was coming back. You're not really going home today?'

A lyrical wave passed over Mr Charlton. With distaste he

remembered his office: the in-tray, the out-tray, the files, the other chaps, the ink-stained desks, the chatter of typewriters.

'If you're sure it's no trouble –'

'Trouble!' Ma said. 'We *want* you. We love to have you.'

'I've finished,' Mariette said. 'Like to get a breath of air?'

Mr Charlton went to the door and stood in the sun. With reviving heart he stared across Pop's paradise of junk, scratching hens, patrols of geese, and graveyards of rusty iron, in the middle of which Montgomery was milking goats under a haystack. Over all this a sky as blue as the thrushes' eggs that had come to disaster in his pocket spread with unblemished purity. The near fringes of meadows had become, overnight, white with moon-daisies, drifts of summer snow. A cuckoo called and was answered by another, the notes like those of tender horns, the birds hidden in oak-trees, among curtains of thickest olive flower.

'How do you feel now?' Mariette said.

The pale face of Mr Charlton broadened into its first unsteady daylight smile.

'A little more perfick than I was.'

*

By Saturday night the deep-freeze was installed. By Sunday morning, three nine-pound geese, well-stuffed with sage and-onion, were sizzling in a pure white electric oven that could have spoken, Mr Charlton thought, if spoke to. A light breeze drove with frailest spinnings of air through the bluebell wood and bore across the hot yard the delicious aroma of roasting birds.

Ma, who loved colour, cooked in a canary yellow pinafore with big scarlet pockets and at intervals shouted across the yard, either to Pop or Mariette, Mr Charlton or the children, or whoever happened to be there, a demand for instructions about the meal.

'What sort of vegetables do you fancy? Asparagus? I got green peas and new potatoes but shout if you want anything different.' It turned out that Montgomery wanted brown braised onions, the twins Yorkshire pudding, and Primrose baked potatoes. 'Fair enough,' Ma said, 'as long as we know.'

At eleven o'clock, by which time Pop was no longer in the yard, Ma shouted that it was already so hot in the kitchen that she'd be sick by the time the meal was served.

'What say we have it outside?' she called. 'Under the walnut tree?'

By noon Mariette, dressed in neat sky-blue linen shorts and an open-necked vermilion blouse, her legs bare, was laying a white cloth on a long table underneath a walnut tree that overshadowed, like a faintly fragrant umbrella, the only civilized stretch of grass near the house, on the south side, beside which Ma would later grow patches of petunia and zinnia, her favourite flowers. It was cool and dark there under the thickening walnut leaves, out of the sun, and Mr Charlton helped her by bringing cutlery from the house on papier-mâché trays brightly decorated with hunting scenes, race-meetings, or pointers carrying birds.

At half past twelve Pop startled everybody by driving into the yard in a Rolls-Royce, a pre-war landaulette in black, with straw-coloured doors that actually looked as if they had been made of plaited basket-work. The horn, sounding with discreet harmonious distinction, brought everybody running to the centre of the rusty, dusty graveyards of junk and iron.

Pop stopped the car and dismounted with triumphant, imperial pride.

'Here it is!' he shouted. 'Ourn!'

Before anyone could speak he leapt down to the doors, proudly pointing.

'Monogram,' he said. 'Look, Ma – monograms on the doors.'

'Royal?' Ma said.

'Duke, I think,' Pop said. 'The feller didn't know. Anyway, duke or viscount or some toff of some sort.'

Ma was dazzled. She took several paces forward and touched the gleaming body-work.

'All in!' Pop said. 'Everybody in! Everybody who wants a ride get in!'

Everybody, including Mr Charlton, got into the Rolls-Royce. On the wide spacious seats of dove-grey upholstery, upon which heavy cords of tasselled yellow silk hung at the windows, there was plenty of room for everybody, but the twins sat on Mr Charlton's lap. Ma herself sat in the centre of the back seat, her pinafore spread out crinoline-wise, almost in royal fashion, her turquoise-ringed hands spread on her yellow pinafore.

Soon an entranced look crept like a web across her face, only her eyes moving as they rolled gently from side to side, taking in the smallest details.

'I wish I had my hat on,' she said at last. 'I don't feel right without my hat on.'

'Got a big picnic basket in the boot,' Pop said. 'Corkscrews an' all.'

'It's got vases for flowers,' Ma said. She leaned forward and fingered with delicacy a pair of silver horn-like vases fixed below the glass screen that divided the back seat from the front.

'Notice anything else?' Pop called. 'Have a good dekko.

All round. Want you to notice one more thing, Ma. Have a good dekko.'

After several seconds of silence, in which Ma's eyes revolved on a slow axis of exploration, in pure wonderment, Ma confessed that she saw nothing more.

'That thing like the bit off the end of a carpet sweeper!' Pop yelled. In his own delight he laughed in his customary ringing fashion. 'Mind it don't bite you.'

'No,' Ma said. 'No.' Her mouth expired air in a long incredulous wheeze. 'No –'

'Speakin' tube!' Pop said. 'Pick it up. Say something down it. Give me order. Say "Home James!" – summat like that.'

Ma, in possession of the end of the speaking tube, sat utterly speechless.

'Give me order!' Pop said. 'I can hear whatever you say perfickly well in front here. Go on, Ma. Give me order!'

Ma breathed into the speaking tube in a voice pitched in a minor key of desolation.

'I don't know whether I like it,' she said. 'They'll be putting the price of fish-and-chips up when they see us roll up in this.'

'Never!' Pop said. 'They'll be paying *us*.'

The receiving end of the speaking apparatus was just above the head of Mr Charlton, who was sitting next to Pop in the driving seat. The voices of Victoria and Primrose began to shriek into his ears like a gabble of excited young ducks.

'Take us for a ride! Take us for a ride! Take us for a ride!'

Pop let in the clutch and started to steer a course of slow elegance between a pile of discarded oil-drums and a big galvanized iron swill-tub. No breath of sound came, for a full minute, from either the Rolls or its passengers.

Then Ma said: 'Like riding on air. Not a squeak anywhere. Must be paid for.'

'Cash down!' Pop said.

He pressed the horn. An orchestration of low notes, harmonious, smooth as honey, disturbed into slight flutterings a batch of young turkeys sunning themselves in the lee of the pig-sties.

'That's the town one,' Pop explained. He flicked a switch with a finger-nail. 'Now hark at this. Country. Open road.'

A peremptory, urgent snarl, like the surprise entry of symphonic brass, tore the peaceful fabric of the yard's livestock to pieces. A whole flotilla of white ducks sprang into the air and raced like hurdlers over rusty junk, empty boxes, and feeding troughs. Brown hens flew like windy paper-bags in all directions, shedding feathers.

'Special fittin',' Pop explained. 'Chap who owned it once lived in Paris or somewheres.'

He completed with slow imperial pride the course of the yard, now blowing the town horn, now the snarl.

'Comfortable in the back, ain't it, Ma? Make a nice bed, don't you think?'

Ma, who had recovered equilibrium, now spoke down the speaking-tube, shaking like a jelly.

'Home, James. Else them geese'll burn.'

Pop responded with the honeyed notes of the town horn and the Rolls, like a ship gliding to anchorage in smooth waters, skirted with a final swing of silent elegance past a strong black alp of pig-manure.

'Perfick, ain't it?' Pop said. 'Ain't it perfick?'

Ma, who had stopped laughing, breathed hard before she spoke again.

'I got to have flowers in the vases,' she said, her voice full of a pleasure so deep that it was at once loving and lovable in humility. 'Every time we go out we got to have flowers.'

Back at the house everybody alighted and Ma once again stroked, with touching affection, the shining chariot wings, her huge body reflected in their black curves with a vast transfiguration of yellow and scarlet, distorted as in a comic mirror at a fair.

'Gorblimey, I must run,' she said suddenly. 'I haven't even started the apple sauce.'

As Ma ran towards the house Mariette remembered the table under the walnut tree and took Mr Charlton's hand. Pop remembered the port and called after a dutifully retreating Mr Charlton:

'Charley boy, like to do summat for me while you're helping Mariette? Put the port on ice, old man, will you? Three bottles. Two red and one white. You'll find two ice buckets in the cocktail cabinet. Give 'em plenty of ice, old man.'

At the same time Montgomery stood staring across the yard in the direction of the road.

'Pop,' he said, 'I think we got a visitor. I think it looks like the Brigadier.'

Across the yard a straight, six-foot human straw was drifting. It was dressed in a suit of tropical alpaca, once yellowish, now bleached to whitish fawn, that looked as if it had recently been under a steam-roller.

It was the Brigadier all right, Pop said, and leaned one hand on the front wing of the Rolls with casual pride, raising the other in greeting. He wondered too what the Brigadier wanted and where his sister was and said he betted the old whippet had left him for the day.

'General!' he called. 'What can I do you for?'

'Hail,' the Brigadier said. The voice was low and cryptic. 'Well met, Larkin.'

At closer range it was to be seen that the Brigadier's elbows had been patched with squares of paler coloured material that appeared to have been torn from pillow-slips. The cuffs of his jacket sleeves had been trimmed more or less level with scissors and then sewn back. His socks were yellow. The hat worn on the back of his head resembled more than anything a frayed bee-skip and seemed to be worn so far back in order to avoid his extraordinary extensive white eyebrows, altogether too large for the rest of his cadaverous face, which stuck above his pale blue eyes like two salty prawns.

These prawns were repeated on his upper lip in stiff moustaches, which contrasted sharply with cheeks consisting entirely of purple veins. The chin was resolute and looked like worn pumice stone. The neck was long and loose and held entirely together by a rigid bolt of fiery crimson, the Adam's apple, which seemed over the course of time to have worn the soiled shirt collar to shreds.

The Brigadier shook hands with Pop, at the same time recognizing in Pop's demeanour the divinity of new possession. He held the Rolls-Royce in flinty stare.

'Not yours?'

'Just got it.'

'Good God.'

Pop made breezy gestures of pride. He wanted instantly to reveal possession of the monograms and then decided against it. It was too much all at one time, he thought.

'Hellish costly to run?'

'Well, might be, can't tell, might be,' Pop said. 'But worth it. Always flog it.'

Sooner or later, in his energetic way, Pop flogged most things.

'Good God.' The Brigadier looked at the car with closer, microscopic inspection. 'What's all this?'

'Monogram.'

'Good God.' In moments of humour the Brigadier drew on dry resources of solemnity. 'No crown?'

The remark was lost on Pop, who was dying to demonstrate the horn's orchestral variations.

'Well,' the Brigadier said, 'I mustn't linger. Down to staff work.'

Pop laughed in his usual ringing fashion and said he betted a quid the General wanted a subscription.

'Wrong,' the Brigadier said. 'Not this time.'

'Well, that's worth a drink,' Pop said. 'What about a snifter?'

'Trifle early, don't you think?' the Brigadier said. 'Not quite over the yard-arm yet, are we?'

'When I want a drink,' Pop said, 'I have a drink. Wevver it's early or wevver it ain't.'

The Brigadier, after a minor pretence at refusal, chose to have a whisky-and-soda. Pop said first that he'd have a Guinness and then changed his mind and said he'd have a beer called Dragon's Blood with a dash of lime instead. The Brigadier looked astonished at this extraordinary combination but followed Pop into the house without a word.

In the sitting-room he found it hard to concentrate even on the whisky-and-soda because of powerful, torturing odours of roasting geese that penetrated every corner of the house, delicious with sage and onion stuffing. He sat most of the time with his glass on his right knee, where it successfully concealed a hole that mice might have gnawed.

66

'Might as well come straight to the point,' the Brigadier said. 'Fact is, Larkin, I'm in a God-awful mess.'

'Wimmin?'

The Brigadier looked extremely startled. The prawns of his eyebrows seemed to leap out. He seemed about to speak and then drank with eagerness at the whisky-and-soda instead.

'No, no, no,' he said eventually. 'Bad enough, but not that bad.'

Pop knew that the Brigadier's sister, who resembled more than anything a long hairpin on the top of which she generally wore a cloche hat that looked like a pink thimble, was presumed to lead him a hell of a dance on most occasions and in all directions. Among other things he felt that she never gave the Brigadier enough to eat: a terrible thing.

'No, it's this damn Gymkhana,' the Brigadier said. 'That Bolshie Fortescue had a God-awful row with the committee Friday and has withdrawn from the field.'

'Always was a basket.'

'Not only withdrawn *from* the field,' the Brigadier said, 'but withdrawn *the* field.'

'Means you've got nowhere to hold the damn thing.'

'Bingo,' the Brigadier said.

In a soft voice Pop called Mr Fortescue a bloody sausage and remembered Mariette. The gymkhana was in a fortnight's time. It might be the last chance she'd ever get to ride in the jumps before she had the baby. She was mad on jumping; her heart was set on horses and all that sort of thing.

'Nothing to worry about,' Pop said. 'You can hold it in my medder.'

'Don't let me rush you into a decision, Larkin,' the Brigadier said. 'You don't have to decide –'

'Good grief,' Pop said. 'Nothing to decide. The medder's there, ain't it? All I got to do is get the grass cut. I'll get the grass cut this week and things'll be perfick.'

The Brigadier was so much touched by this that he nervously held his glass in his left hand and started poking a finger into the hole in his right trouser knee, a habit about which his sister had already scolded him acidly twice at breakfast.

'Can't thank you enough, Larkin,' he said. He several times used the words 'eternal gratitude' in low muttered voice, as in prayer. He coughed, drank again, poked at the hole in his knee, and called Pop a stout feller. He knew the committee would be eternally grateful. 'Never be able to thank you.'

Out of politeness he rose to go. Before he was on his feet Pop was insisting on another snifter and Ma, hearing the tinkle of ice in glasses, called from the kitchen:

'What about one for the old cook in here? What's she done today?'

The Brigadier, under indeterminate protest, had a second whisky-and-soda. Pop had a change of mind and had a whisky-and-soda too. Ma ordered beer because she was parched from cooking and came to the sitting-room door to drink it from a big glass that spilled foam down her hands.

'Bung-ho,' she said to the Brigadier. 'How's your sister today?'

'Gone to see an aunt,' the Brigadier said. Now that Ma had opened the kitchen door the smell of browning goose-flesh was attacking him in even more frontal, more excruciating waves. 'Over in Hampshire. Day's march away.'

'Sunday dinner all on your lonesome?' Ma said.

'Not quite that bad.' Torturing waves of sage-sharp fragrance from the roasting geese made him suddenly feel more heady than even the whisky-and-soda had done on his empty stomach. 'I shall waffle down to the pub and grab a bite of cold.'

'Cold on Sundays?' Ma was deeply shocked. 'You wouldn't catch Pop having cold on Sundays. Why don't you stay here and eat with us?'

'No, no, really no. No, thanks all the same, really –'

'Encore,' Pop said. 'More the merrier. Perfick.'

'Bless my soul, with all your brood –'

'Of course,' Ma said. 'Cold, my foot.'

'Ma,' Pop said, 'pity you didn't put that leg o' pork in after all.' Ma had calculated that, within reason, three nine-pound geese ought to be enough. 'Too late now I suppose?'

He seemed quite disappointed as Ma said, 'Not unless you want to eat about five o'clock,' and went away kitchenwards. He hated having to skimp on joints and things; it made it hard work for the carver.

From the kitchen Ma called a minute later:

'Come here a minute, Pop, I want you. Lift the geese out of the oven for me, will you? I want to baste them.'

Pop went into the kitchen, realizing as soon as he went through the door that the call was after all merely a ruse to get him away from the Brigadier. Ma was standing by the window, arms folded like huge white vegetable marrows across her bolstered bosom, looking towards the walnut tree.

'Take a look at that,' she said.

Under the tree, at the dinner table, cloth and cutlery having been laid, Mariette and Mr Charlton were coolly sitting some distance apart from each other, absorbed in the Sunday papers.

Ma made noises of puzzled disgust, which Pop echoed.

'What's wrong with 'em?'

'Wrong? Don't he know his technique?' Ma said.

'Very like do better on the boat this afternoon,' Pop said. 'There's some very good quiet places up the river.'

Ma, as if she could not bear the sight any longer, turned away to stir the apple sauce with a wooden spoon as it simmered away in a new bright aluminium pan. After looking at it critically she decided it needed a touch of something and dropped into the steaming olive-yellow purée a lump of butter as big as a tennis ball.

'Brigadier looks seedy, I think, don't you?' she said. Pop agreed. He felt immensely sorry for the Brigadier. 'Trouble with these people they never get enough to eat. Like Mr Charlton. Half-starved.'

Pop agreed with that too. 'Cold at the pub Sundays,' he said, as if this was the depths of deplorable gastronomic misery. 'Can you beat it?'

Ma said she could. 'Because if I know anything about it he wasn't going near the pub. He was going home to a Marmite sandwich and a glass o' milk. Perhaps even water.'

A moment later she turned to reach from a cupboard a new tin of salt and Pop, watching her upstretched figure as it revealed portions of enormous calves, suddenly felt a startling twinge of excitement in his veins. He immediately grasped Ma by the bosom and started squeezing her. Ma pretended to protest, giggling at the same time, but Pop continued to fondle her with immense, experienced enthusiasm, until finally she turned, yielded the great continent of her body to him and let him kiss her full on her soft big mouth.

Pop prolonged this delicious experience as long as he had breath. He always felt more passionate in the kitchen. He supposed it was the smell of food. Ma sometimes told him it was a wonder he ever got any meals at all and that he ought to know, at his age, which he wanted most, meals or her. 'Both,' he always said. 'Often.'

This morning, against the shining white stove, the glistening aluminium pans and the background of sunlight on the young coppery green leaves of the walnut tree, he thought she looked absolutely lovely. She was his dream.

He started to kiss her passionately again. But this time she held him away. The Brigadier, she said, would be wondering what was happening. He was to go back to the Brigadier. 'The twins'll be back with the ice-cream any moment too,' she said. The twins had gone to the village, a quarter of a mile down the road, with orders to bring back the largest blocks of strawberry and chocolate *mousse* they could buy.

'Take the Brigadier a few crisps,' Ma said. 'They'll keep him going for half an hour.'

With reluctance Pop went back to the Brigadier, who sat staring into an empty glass, elbows on his knees, his trouser legs hitched up so that his socks and thin hairy shins were revealed. Pop saw now that the socks were odd, one yellow and one white, and that both had potatoes in the heels.

'Crisp, General?' he said and held out a big plastic orange dish of potato crisps, glistening fresh and salty.

The Brigadier, who belonged to two London clubs that he used only twice a year and spent most of the rest of his time wearing himself to a skeleton chopping wood, washing dishes, clipping hedges, mowing the lawn, and cleaning out blocked drainpipes because he couldn't afford a man, accepted the crisps with formal reluctance that actually concealed a boyish gratitude.

Pop also suggested another snifter.

'No, no. Thanks all the same. No, no,' the Brigadier said. 'No really,' and then allowed his glass to be taken away from him with no more than dying stutters of protestation.

Half an hour later two of the three geese were lying side by side, browned to perfection, deliciously varnished with running gravy, in a big oval blue meat dish on the table under the walnut tree. Other blue dishes stood about the table containing green peas and new potatoes veined with dark sprigs of mint, baked onions, asparagus, roast potatoes, Yorkshire pudding, and broad beans in parsley sauce. There were also big blue boats of apple sauce and gravy.

There had been times in his life when the Brigadier would have been prompted, out of sheer good form, social constraint, and various other preventive forces of up-bringing, to describe the sight of all this as rather lacking in decency. Today he merely sat with restrained bewilderment, tortured by odours of goose-flesh and sage-and-onions, watching the faces of Pop, Ma, Mister Charlton, and the entire Larkin brood while Pop carved with dextrous ease at the birds, themselves not at all unlike brown laden galleons floating in a glistening gravy sea.

Even the stiff prawns of his eyebrows made no quiver of surprise as Pop, flashing carving knife and steel in air, suggested that if Charley boy wanted to help he could pour the port out now.

Mr Charlton put the port on the table in its champagne bucket, all beady with icy dew.

'Mix it,' Pop said. 'It makes a jolly good drink, red and white mixed together.'

Mr Charlton went round the table, pouring and mixing port. He had been introduced to the Brigadier by a more than usually facetious Pop as 'a late entry – chap on the tax lark'.

'Actually a real pukka tax-gatherer you mean?' the Brigadier said, as if astonished that there could be such a person.

'Inspector's office,' Mr Charlton said.

'Tried to rope *me* in on that swindle yesterday,' Pop said. He laughed derisively, in his customary ringing fashion. 'I should like, eh, General? What do you say?'

The Brigadier confessed, with a certain sadness, that he paid no tax. At least, hardly any.

'And rightly so!' Pop thundered.

Succulent pieces of bird were now being carved and dispatched about the table with breezy speed.

'That all right for you, General?' The Brigadier found himself facing an entire leg of goose and a large mound of sage-and-onions.

'Start!' Pop ordered. 'Don't let it get cold, General!' To the goose Mariette came to add peas, beans, Yorkshire pudding, and two sorts of potatoes, so that finally, when gravy and apple sauce had been ladled on, no single centimetre of naked plate could be seen.

A moment later the Brigadier, faced with superior forces and not knowing where to attack, saw Ma, like some huge yellow and scarlet butterfly glowing in the walnut shade, come up on his flank, bearing a deep dish of fat and buttery asparagus. With dry humour he started to confess to being out-numbered, a problem that Ma at once solved by placing the dish between the Brigadier and the head of table, where she herself now sat down.

'We'll share, shall we, General?' she said. 'Help yourself from the dish. Everybody else has had some.'

It was some moments before the Brigadier, deeply touched and painfully strung up by the first delicious tortures of eating, could relax enough to remember formality and lift his glass to Ma.

'Mr Charlton, I think we should raise a glass to our hostess.'

''Ear, 'ear,' Pop said. 'Cheers to Ma.'

The Brigadier bent upwards from the table, raising his glass to Ma. Mr Charlton also half-rose and raised his glass and at the same moment Victoria said, pointing to the Brigadier:

'You got potatoes in your socks, I saw them.'

'Now, now,' Pop said. 'Manners. Elbows!'

Victoria was silent.

'Pop's got 'em at a word,' Ma said proudly. 'And now *eat* your potatoes,' she said to Victoria. 'Never mind about the General's.'

'This is most superb cooking,' the Brigadier said. 'Where did you learn to cook, Mrs Larkin?'

'She learned at *The Three Cocks* hotel at Fordington,' Pop said. 'That's where she learnt. I can tell you. And it's never been the same since she left there.'

'I can only say the cock's loss is your gain,' the Brigadier said, a remark that Ma found so amusing that she started choking again, her mouth jammed by a piece of asparagus.

'Hit her, General!' Pop said. 'Middle o' the back!'

The Brigadier was utterly startled by this sudden and unnatural order. He moved vaguely to action by putting down his knife and fork, but a second later Ma had recovered.

'All right, Ma?' Pop said. 'Drink a drop o' wine.'

Ma, sipping wine, said thanks, she was all right again.

'Ma's got a very small gullet,' Pop explained to the Brigadier, 'compared with the rest of her.'

'Have you told the children about the Gymkhana, Larkin?' the Brigadier said.

'Good God, went clean out of my head,' Pop said. Waving a dripping wing-bone, which he had been busily sucking for some moments past, he informed the entire table in proud, imperial tones: 'Going to hold the Gymkhana in the medder, kids. *Here*.'

Before anyone could speak an excited Mariette was on her feet, running round the table to Pop, whom she began kissing with great fervour on the lips, hardly a degree less passionately than Pop, in the kitchen, had kissed Ma.

'Lovely, lovely man. Lovely, lovely Pop.'

Mr Charlton sat tremulous, completely shaken. A curious wave of emotion, at first hot, then cold, lapped entirely through him from the small of his back to his brain. Unaccountably he found himself both jealous, then afraid, of the unquenchable demonstration that had left Pop, laughing loudly, hugging Mariette in return. He was not used to unquenchable demonstrations.

'That's the loveliest, loveliest news. Don't you think so, Mr Charlton?'

'You should really thank the General,' Pop said. 'His idea.'

'Committee –'

The word had hardly broken from the lips of the Brigadier before Mariette was at his side, kissing him too. The Brigadier, looking formally delighted, began to wipe his mouth with his serviette, but whether to wipe away kiss or asparagus butter it was not possible to say. He was still dabbing his mouth when Mariette kissed Ma, who explained to the Brigadier: 'Mad on horses, General. Absolutely stark raving mad on horses,' and then came round the table to where Mr Charlton sat concentrating with every nerve on scraping the last tissues of goose-flesh from a leg bone.

Mr Charlton was all mixed up. He was fighting to concentrate. He was fighting to disentangle one thought, one fear, from another. There had crossed his mind, for no sensible reason at all, the uneasy notion that the goose he was now eating might well be part of the same living bird that had so sinuously, shimmeringly wrapped its neck about his legs the previous day, with the shattering sensation of their being caressed by silk stockings. It was the most disturbing thought of his life and he knew that he was blushing. He knew he was afraid.

'Oh! Mr Charlton, I'm so happy I think I'll kiss you too.'

Mariette, to the unconcealed delight and satisfaction of Ma and Pop, bent and kissed Mr Charlton briefly, but with purpose, full on the lips. Mr Charlton recoiled in a crimson cloud, hearing about him trumpets of disaster. Everyone was laughing.

When he came to himself he knew he could never forget that moment. He was trembling all over. It was impossible to describe what the full soft lips of Mariette had felt like against his own except that it was, perhaps, like having them brushed by the skin of a warm firm plum, in full ripeness, for the first time.

While Mr Charlton was still blushing Pop retired to the kitchen and fetched another goose. He began to carve for the Brigadier several thin extra-succulent slices of the breast. This one, he started saying, as he slid the knife across the crackling dark golden skin, was the tenderest of them all and a moment later confirmed Mr Charlton's worst fears by laughing uproariously:

'This must be the joker that was under the table yesterday and heard us talking. Eh, Ma? Think o' that.'

'Knowing birds,' Ma said and turned to the Brigadier to ask: 'What was it you was going to say, General, about the Committee?'

'Oh! merely that I was elected to be spokesman. To ask your husband –'

'Who's on the Committee?' Ma said.

'Well, Edith is secretary. Edith Pilchester. I expect she'll be coming to see you.'

'Oh! I love old Edith,' Pop said. 'Edith's a sport.'

'You be careful she don't love you,' Ma said. 'I wouldn't put anything past her.'

'Ah! perfickly harmless,' Pop said.

'Splendid organizer,' the Brigadier said.

'That's what she thinks. She fancies she could organize a stallion into having pups,' Ma said, 'but that's where she's wrong,' and once again, as she did so often at her own jokes, laughed with jellified splendour.

'Then there's Mrs Peele and George Carter,' the Brigadier said.

'Still living together I suppose?' Ma said.

'I understand the arrangement still holds.'

'Disgusting.'

Ma made tutting noises as she sucked a final piece of asparagus. Pop belched with sudden richness and said 'Manners.' It was terrible the way people carried on, Ma said and Pop agreed.

'Then there's Freda O'Connor.'

'She's another tart if you like,' Ma said. 'Showing off her bosom.'

'And Jack Woodley.'

'That feller's another So-and-so,' Pop said. 'Just like Fortescue. A complete b – '

'Not in front of the twins,' Ma said. 'I don't mind Victoria. She's not old enough to understand.'

'And then Mrs Borden. That makes the lot.'

Ma, eating the last of her peas with a tablespoon, made more noises of disgust and asked if Mrs Borden was still keeping as sober as ever? Supposed she was?

'With the same fish-like capacity I understand,' the Brigadier said.

'Terrible,' Ma said. 'Shocking. Terrible state of affairs when you let drink get you down like that.'

'Disgusting,' Pop said. 'Disgusting.'

It was time for ice-cream. Mariette rose to fetch it from the kitchen, together with a jug of real Jersey, hoping that Mr Charlton would seize so good an opportunity and come with her, but Mr Charlton was still all mixed up. The day had grown exceptionally humid and warm, the air thick with the stirring breath of growing leaves and grasses. Mariette felt the sweetness of it tingling madly in her nostrils and remembered the kiss she had given Mr Charlton. She was sorry for Mr Charlton and wondered if it would ever be possible to make love with him. Making love might ease his mind. In the meadow beyond the house she had noticed how high the buttercups were growing, thick and sappy and golden among the grasses' feathery flower, and she wondered what it would be like to make love to Mr Charlton in a buttercup field. She thought she could but try. She was growing fonder and fonder of Mr Charlton. His eyes were soft, endearing, and sometimes even sad and she found herself fascinated by their brown, delicate paintbrush lashes.

'Cuppa tea, General?'

After the ice-cream Ma was sitting back with a great air of content, as if really getting ready to enjoy herself.

'No, no, no. No really, thank you.'

'No trouble. Always have one after dinner.'

The thought of tea after two plates of goose, asparagus, sage-and-onions, ice-cream, and everything else provoked in the Brigadier's stomach a restless thunderstorm. He suppressed a belch of his own. Pop was not so successful and a positive bark leapt out, causing Primrose to say:

'I love sage-and-onions. You keeping having a taste of it all afternoon. And sometimes all night too.'

Mariette went away to the house to make tea, hoping again that Mr Charlton would go with her, but Mr Charlton was still battling for courage and concentration. Ma hoped so too and made pointed remarks about the heaviness of cups and trays. Mr Charlton, soporific as well as fearful, made no hint of a move and Ma gave it all up, at last, in disgust. He just didn't know his technique, that was all.

When at last Mariette came across the garden with the tea the Brigadier was moved to admiration of the dark, delicious little figure advancing with shapely provocation under the pure hot light of early afternoon.

'Remarkably pretty she looks,' he told Ma, who agreed with surprisingly energetic warmth, saying:

'I'm glad somebody thinks so. She's been hiding her light under a bushel long enough.'

'Well, I don't know', Pop said, 'as you can say that.' He was thinking of the news Ma had told him two days before. Well, he supposed it was hiding her light in a way. Keeping it dark, anyway.

Everybody except the Brigadier had tea, which Mariette poured out thick and strong, with Jersey cream. To Mr Charlton's surprise nobody suggested Johnny Walker milk, though Pop stirred into his own cup two teaspoonfuls of port. It was still icy.

'Helps to cool it down,' he explained. 'Ma can't do with it in a saucer.'

An afternoon of delicious golden content folded its transparent envelope more and more softly about the paradisiacal Larkin world, over the outlying meadow scintillating with its million buttercups and the shady fragrant walnut tree. Pop sighed and remarked how perfick it was. If only the Gymkhana was as perfick it would be marvellous, he said. Should they have fireworks? 'Tell the Committee I'll provide the fireworks,' he said to the Brigadier. 'That'll make it go with a bang.'

The Brigadier, who did not answer, was almost asleep. The twins and the younger children had already slipped away. Ma was falling slowly asleep too, her head falling sideways, so that she was now less like a bright expansive butterfly than a vast yellow parrot tucking its head under its sleepy wing.

'Look at that sky, Charley,' Pop said and indicated with the tip of an unlighted cigar the exquisite expanse of all heaven, blue as flax-flower. 'There's summat worth while for you. Perfick. Blimey, I wonder how you fellers can work in offices.'

Mr Charlton was beginning to wonder too.

'Cigar?'

Mr Charlton declined the cigar with low thanks.

'Ought to have given the General one,' Pop said. The Brigadier was now fast asleep. Bad manners to have forgot the General, he thought. He liked the General. The old sport might not live very grand but he was unmistakably a gent. Not like George Carter and Jack Woodley and a few other baskets he could name. Nor Freda O'Connor and Mrs Battersby and Molly Borden and that crowd. They didn't think much of people like him and Ma. That's why they'd sent the General along as spokesman. He knew.

He liked Edith Pilchester though. Edith was a sport. He laughed softly as he thought that if they had fireworks at the Gymkhana he would put one under Edith's skirts, just to see what happened. 'Probably never turn a hair,' he thought. 'Probably get a thrill.'

'Put the cigar on the General's plate, Charley,' he said to Mr Charlton, 'when you get round to going.'

'I think we're going now,' Mariette said to Mr Charlton, 'aren't we?'

Mr Charlton, who had been in a mix-up all afternoon, abruptly fumbled to his feet, expressing agreement by taking the cigar and laying it beside the Brigadier's head, reclining now in flushed oblivion on the table.

'Going on the boat?' Pop said.

'Might do,' Mariette said. 'Might not get that far.'

'Perfick anyway,' Pop said, 'wherever you go.'

As they crossed from the garden to the big meadow beyond Mariette took Mr Charlton's hand. In the startled fashion of a young colt he almost jumped as she touched him. A wave of fragrance blew on the lightest breath of wind from the direction of the river, driving into her quickening nostrils odours of hawthorn bloom, clover, an entire valley of rising grasses, and distant invisible fields of early may.

It was so exquisitely strong that suddenly she bent down, took off her shoes, and started running.

A moment later, Mr Charlton, running too, realized how pretty, how exciting, her naked feet were.

5

THAT evening Pop, after a half hour of twilight spent with Ma in the bluebell wood, listening to a whole orchestra of nightingales, came back to the house to urge on Mr Charlton the virtues of a little sick leave.

'Ma and me don't think you look all that grand,' he said.

Ma followed this up by saying that she didn't like the look round Mr Charlton's cheek-bones. There were white spots on them. White spots were a bad sign, but of what she didn't say.

Pop went on to urge on Mr Charlton to use his loaf and take proper advantage of what he called 'the National Elf lark', a service which, after all, Mr Charlton paid for. Pop was certain Mr Charlton had already paid out millions to this swindle in weekly contributions. It must have cost him a fortune in stamps. With warmth he urged Mr Charlton not to be a mug about it. It was, after all, the State that had started this lark – why not go sick, he urged, and have a bit of fun?

Mr Charlton might have resisted these arguments if it hadn't been that, just before midnight, Mariette pinned him up against the newel post of the dark stairs, kissed him again, and said his hands were hot. Like white spots on the cheek-bones, hot hands were a bad sign. Mr Charlton tried to protest that his hands were invariably hot, especially at that time of year, but Mariette kissed him again, pressing her warm plum-like mouth for a long time against his lips, leaving him in another terrible turmoil of divided emotions about the buttercup field, the nightingales, and the affair of the goose-neck entwining his leg.

'You could stay a week, lovey,' she said. She had begun to call him lovey in the buttercup field. 'And then all next week-end.'

Mr Charlton tried to explain that he had a vast and frightful number of papers on his desk at the office that had to be attended to and how there would be an awful stink if he didn't get back.

'Think if you broke your leg,' she said.

Mr Charlton said he didn't want to think of breaking his leg. He was talking about loyalty, duty, pangs of conscience, and that sort of thing.

'Sounds silly,' Mariette said and Mr Charlton, trembling on the dark stairs, under the influence of the pressing, plum-like lips, was bound to admit that it did.

The result was that he got up next morning to a massive breakfast of two fried eggs, several slices of liver and bacon, much fried bread, and enormous cups of black sugary tea.

Pop was already breakfasting when he arrived at table. Poised heartily above a sea of tomato-ketchup, under which whatever he was having for breakfast was completely submerged, he praised for some moments the utter beauty of the first young strawberry morning. It was going to be a perfick day, he said. The cuckoo had been calling since four o'clock.

The only thing that troubled Mr Charlton as he ate his breakfast was that he felt there was absolutely nothing wrong with him. He could honestly complain of neither sickness nor exhaustion. He had never felt better. 'I don't know what to tell the office,' he said. 'Honestly there's nothing wrong with me.'

'Then you must make summat up,' Pop said, 'mustn't you? Like lumbago.'

Mr Charlton protested that he had never had lumbago in his life, and was not likely to have.

'Oh! yes you are,' Pop said and laughed in hearty, ringing fashion. 'You'll have it chronic tonight. After the first day in the strawberry field.'

At eight o'clock Mr Charlton found himself sitting in the back of the gentian-blue, home-painted truck, together with Mariette, the twins, Montgomery, Victoria, and Primrose. Ma and Pop sat in the cab in front and Ma, who was in great spirits and was dressed in enormous khaki denim slacks with an overall top, laughed and said it was a pity they couldn't all go in the Rolls, just to shake everybody. Mariette was in slacks too, bright salvia red ones, with a soft blue shirt and a spotted red-and-white kerchief over her hair. Over the khaki overalls Ma was wearing the salmon jumper, just because the ride might be cool in the morning air, and a great pudding-bag of an orange scarf on her head.

'Everybody all right in the back there?' Pop yelled and got his customary handsome ribbon of voices in answer. 'Hang on by your toe-nails you kids!'

The truck had hardly rolled out of the yard before everyone began singing. It was Pop who started the song, which was *We Ain't Got a Barrel o' Money*, and everyone took it up in shrill voices. Mr Charlton was embarrassed. He had never ridden in the back of a truck before. Still less had he ever sung in a truck on a public highway.

He wondered what on earth would happen if he was seen by someone who knew him, someone perhaps from the office. It would be terrible to be seen by any of the chaps.

Half a mile down the road the truck drew up with a sharp whistle of brakes and everyone stopped singing and started shrieking loudly instead. Mr Charlton looked over the sideboard of the truck to see what the trouble was and saw Pop in the road, lifting up in his arms the tiniest woman Mr Charlton had, outside a circus, ever seen.

'Room for a little 'un?' Pop said and threw the little lady up into the truck. She shrieked like a laughing doll as she landed between the twins and Mr Charlton. 'That Little Two-penn'orth', Pop explained, 'is Aunt Fan.'

Aunt Fan to whom? Mr Charlton wondered but never discovered. His immediate impression was that The Little Two-penn'orth had a face like a small brown shell-fish of the winkle sort. It was all round and crinkled and twisted up. She too was wearing slacks, tiny dark maroon red ones, and a man's grey tweed cap on her head, fixed there by two large pearl hat-pins. Her ginger-brown eyes shone like shoe-buttons and her chest was flat.

'Everybody all right in the truck there? Hang on, Aunt Fan!'

Once again everybody, including The Little Two-penn'orth, started singing. By this time the sun was well above the miles of surrounding orchards, chestnut copses, and fields of rising oats and barley, and as it shone down on the truck and on the laughing, singing faces, Mr Charlton saw a tiny creature popping in and out of Aunt Fan's mouth, exactly like a pink mollusc emerging from its shell. This was The Little Two-penn'orth's tongue and it helped to work the shrillest voice he had ever heard. It was a voice like a wild train-whistle shrieking to be heard on a far mountain top.

'Don't you sing, mister?' she said.

Mr Charlton, grinning feebly, did not know what to say. His hair was flying about in all directions. The truck was wildly bumping over a hard clay track, jolting Aunt Fan and the children to new laughter. Mr Charlton did sing. He flattered himself, excusably, that he sang rather well. His voice, belying his bony, very average physique, was a deep, soft baritone. But now his mouth and throat felt like pumice-stone and he was not sure, with the wild bouncing of the truck, quite where his breakfast was.

'You're new, ainyer?' The Little Two-penn'orth said.

Mr Charlton confessed that he was new.

'Thought you was. On 'oliday?'

'Sort of,' Mr Charlton said.

Another mile of this, he thought, and he wouldn't need an excuse for the National Health lark. His breakfast would be up.

To his great relief the truck came to a halt, two minutes later, between a copse of tall chestnut saplings and a big open strawberry field. A sudden sensation of dizziness found Mr Charlton unready as he jumped from the truck. He groped at the air and was suddenly surprised to see The Little Two-penn'orth flying down from the back of the truck, straight into his arms.

He clasped at the toy-like body instinctively, as at a ball. The Little Two-penn'orth landed straight on his chest, winding him temporarily. Everyone began laughing and The Little Two-penn'orth shrieked with delight. Ma started shaking like a jelly and Pop warned Mr Charlton that he'd better watch out or else Aunt Fan would have him on the floor in no time.

'Just what I'd like on a nice warm day,' The Little Two-penn'orth said. 'Just what I bin waiting for.'

Mr Charlton did his best to focus the shimmering strawberry field. He was now convinced that a terrible day lay in front of him. The sun was clear and hot under the shelter of the barrier of woodland; by noon it would be blistering down. Yesterday had been the hottest thirtieth of May, so the papers all said, for forty years. Today would be hotter even than that.

'You can eat all the strawberries you like,' Mariette said. 'But you'll soon get tired of that.'

Mr Charlton did not feel at all like eating strawberries. He longed to be able to sit down, if possible to lie down, in some cool quiet place under the chestnut saplings.

'Keep near me,' Mariette said and gave him a dark low stare which he was too sick to appreciate or return.

He followed her, the rest of the family, and The Little Two-penn'orth into the strawberry field. Already, along the yellow alleys of straw, twenty or thirty girls and women, with an odd man or two, were picking. Flag-wise a strange assortment of shirts and blouses, yellow and red and green and brown and even violet, was strung about the field. A green canvas tent, towards which Mr Charlton looked with pitiful desperation, as at an oasis, stood in the centre of the field, piled about with fresh white chip baskets.

Bending down, Mr Charlton started to pick strawberries, deciding at the same time that he would never again eat pig's liver and bacon for breakfast. The hot summery distances were full of calling cuckoos. The field trembled like a zither with chattering women's voices. A man decided to strip his shirt off and the sudden sight of his pure naked torso set every female voice laughing, cat-calling, or simply whistling in admiring wonder.

'Why don't you do that, lovey?' Mariette said. 'You'd be all that much cooler. In time you'd get marvellously brown.'

'I think I'll try and get acclimatized first,' Mr Charlton said.

The process of getting acclimatized took him through a sickening forty minutes of sweat. His spectacles misted over. The Little Two-penn'orth's voice, piercing as a drill, cut the hot air about him, as it seemed, every several seconds. Broad belts of Ma's quivering laughter slapped across the field.

Lying on their fresh beds of straw, the squarish fat crimson strawberries shone in the sun with a too-perfect beauty: exactly, as Pop said, as if painted, and now and then Mr Charlton looked up to see the lips of Mariette parted half in laughter, half in the act of biting into some glistening arc of lovely dark ripe flesh.

'Heavens, I'm getting hungry,' she told him several times. 'I hope Ma brought the rest of the cold roast goose for dinner.'

He was very slow, he presently discovered, at the picking. Mariette could fill, with swift deft ease, three punnet-baskets to his one.

'You're not very fast, are you?' she said. 'Don't you feel very well?'

Mr Charlton confessed with a small wry smile that he was not quite a top note.

'I thought as much,' she said. 'It's just what we were telling you yesterday. You need some sick leave. Come on – let's go along to the tent and get the baskets weighed. You have to get them weighed and checked there.'

It turned out that this, the tent, was Mr Charlton's salvation. Pop, who was also at the tent getting his first baskets checked, introduced him to the foreman, a youngish energetic man in khaki shirt and slacks, as 'Charley boy. Friend of ours, Mr Jennings. Office feller from the tax-lark.'

Mr Jennings appraised Mr Charlton, of the tax-lark, with interested swiftness. You didn't often get office fellers in the strawberry field.

'Chap I'm looking for,' he told Mr Charlton. 'What about sitting here and doing my job? All you do is weigh and book the baskets. How about it? I got a million things to do besides sit here and check these ruddy women.'

'There y'are, Charley boy,' Pop said, clapping him on the shoulder and laughing in ringing fashion. 'Got you promoted already.'

Mr Charlton felt intensely relieved. To his astonishment Pop shook his hand.

'Well: got to run along now, Charley boy. Got to see a man about some scrap iron. Don't do anything I wouldn't do. See you all about five.'

Pop departed across the field to the truck and Mr Charlton, sitting down at the table in the green shade of the tent, at once felt much more himself, much more at home. With a chair under his bottom it was almost like being back in the office again.

'It's pretty simple,' Mr Jennings said, and went on to explain what he said was the easy, straightforward procedure of checking, weighing, and recording the baskets. Mr Charlton thought it was simple too. 'Nothing to it,' Mr Jennings said. 'You just got to keep a record in the book here, with the names, that's all, so we can pay out at the end of the day.'

Mr Jennings departed too after saying that he'd come back in an hour or so to see how Mr Charlton was getting on, though he didn't think, on the whole, he'd have any trouble at all.

'One or two of the old faggots might try a bit of cheek on you,' he said, 'but if they do, be firm. Don't let 'em spit in your eye.'

Mr Charlton said he thought he had it taped all right and sat back and cleaned his glasses and combed his hair. Across the field he could see all kinds of women, fat ones, scrawny ones, pretty ones, old ones, very young ones, together with children, bending and laughing in the long strawberry rows, their blouses and slacks stringing out flag-wise, in brilliant colours, under a hot cloudless sky. It was a very pleasant, peaceful, pastoral scene, he thought, and there was a delicious fragrance of ripe strawberries in the air.

'Forgotten me?'

He was startled. He had utterly forgotten Mariette, who had been standing behind him all the time.

'Afraid I had. So absorbed in the new job and all that –'

'Well, don't,' she said, 'or I'll be miserable.' She kissed him lightly on the cheek. 'Feeling better now?'

'Absolutely all right.'

'You see, I told you,' she said. 'All you want is rest and fresh air and good food and you'll be as right as rain.'

She stood at the door of the tent, so prettily framed against the clear sky beyond that Mr Charlton wished he were back with her in the buttercup field.

'See you soon,' she said. 'And mind what you're up to. Don't get mixed up with other women.'

Mr Charlton, who had no intention whatsoever of getting mixed up with other women, started to apply himself earnestly to the task of checking and weighing the baskets of fruit as they came in. It seemed that he got on very well for a time. All the women seemed very polite and some actually called him 'Duckie'. They spelt their names out carefully when he wasn't quite sure of them. They said how hot it was and one of them, a big sloppy woman named Poll Sanders, with gold-filled teeth and small gold earrings, laughed in a voice like a street-trader selling mackerel and said:

'Sweat – I can feel it running down my back. Goes on like this we'll have to strip out again – like we did that 'ot year afore. Remember that, Lil?'

Lil remembered. 'And that wasn't as 'ot as this though.' Lil was tall, yellow, and hollow-faced. She too had small gold earrings. She was much thinner than Poll but this made no difference. She sweated as much as Poll did. 'Runs orf yer like water.'

Mr Charlton wrote in the book that Poll Sanders had brought in two dozen baskets and then, looking up, saw that Lil had gone. He realized suddenly that he had forgotten exactly how many baskets Lil had brought in. He dropped his rubber-tipped pencil on the table and ran after her, catching her up twenty yards across the field.

He said he was frightfully sorry but he had forgotten the number of baskets.

She gave him a look as hard as flint and her mouth opened and shut like a spring trap.

'Two dozen,' she said.

'That's what I thought,' he said and she gave him another look, harder than the first, and he left it at that.

'You want to get your arithmetic working,' she said.

His arithmetic wasn't working very well with Poll Sanders either. When he got back to the tent and sat down to write Lil's figures he discovered he had pencilled down three for Poll Sanders instead of two. Poll had disappeared.

He was so sure the figure was two that he ran after her too.

'Three,' she said. She too gave him that same flat, unflinching look he had seen on the face of Lil. 'I was standing there when you writ it down, wasn't I? Use your loaf, man.'

He decided he'd better use his loaf as much as possible, but he was soon over-busy and it was very stifling in the little tent. He had to keep a sharper, keener eye on the figures as the women came in, bringing scores of baskets. Once The Little Two-penn'orth came in, bent double by two dozen baskets in boxes almost as large as herself, so that they hung from her little hands like overladen panniers from the sides of a tiny grey donkey. The entire Larkin family also came in, all of them eating potato-crisps and big orange lollipops on sticks, except the twins, who were eating pea-nuts, strawberries, and bread-and-jam.

Ma offered Mr Charlton an orange lollipop on a stick and seemed surprised, even pained, when he said no thanks, he didn't think so.

'You'll be glad of it,' she said. 'You ain't had nothing since breakfast.' Mr Charlton still had moments when he found it impossible to remember breakfast with anything but pain. 'Anyway I'll leave it here on the table. You might be glad of it later.'

'Toodle-oo,' the twins said, 'if you don't want it we'll eat it next time we come,' and ran after Ma, begging for ice-creams.

Mr Charlton looked up, sometime later, to see a pretty, fair-haired, well-made girl standing in the tent. She was wearing tight black jeans and an even tighter thin black woollen sweater. The outlines of her breasts under the sweater were as pronounced as if carved. Her hair was tied up in a long shining horse-tail, the fluffy sun-whitened ends of it brushing her bare shoulders.

'Pauline Jackson,' she said, 'two dozen.'

Her eyes were big and blue. Her very smooth skin was deep brown from working in the fields. Her forearms were covered with tender, downy golden hairs. Her tongue played on her straight white teeth when she had finished speaking.

While Mr Charlton was writing in the book she said:

'New here, aren't you? Never seen you here before.'

'Sort of on holiday,' Mr Charlton explained.

'Nice to be some people.'

She had a slow, drowsy way of talking. It somehow matched the way her tongue remained playing on her lips and the way her hair fell on her shoulders.

'Mind if I ask you something?' she said.

'No,' Mr Charlton said. 'What would that be?'

'Is your name Cedric? They all say your name's Cedric out there.'

The blush that ramped through Mr Charlton's face and neck made every pore of his body break with sweat.

'Oh! no,' he said. 'Goodness, no. Who told you that one?'

'That's what they all say. I said there was no such name.'

She was laughing at him, he thought, in her drowsy, large-eyed way. He was sure of that. He fumbled about nervously with book, baskets, and papers and said:

'Good Lord, no. Charley. That's me.'

She reached out a brown long-fingered hand and took a strawberry from a basket. She bit into it and then stood staring at the white-crimson juicy inner flesh.

'Don't you like strawberries?' she said.

'Ask the Larkins,' he said. 'Ask Mariette. They all call me Charley.'

'Oh! her. She knows you, does she?'

She put the rest of the strawberry in her mouth and pulled out the clean, white plug.

'Last feller who was here did nothing but eat strawberries. Every time you came in here that feller was bolting straw-berries.'

Mr Charlton, confused again, murmured something about having no time. Having something else to do.

'Such as what?'

Mr Charlton didn't know.

She moved nearer the table to pick up another strawberry and then changed her mind and picked up Ma's orange lollipop instead.

'Don't you like these either?'

'Not frightfully –'

'Don't like anything, do you?' She laughed, her voice drowsier than ever in her throat, the tongue drifting idly across her mouth. 'Not much!'

A moment later she started twisting the lollipop round and round in her brown fingers.

'Suppose you'd think I was greedy if I asked you whether I could have it?'

'Oh! no please,' Mr Charlton said. 'Take it if you want. By all means.'

'Thanks.' She laughed again, once more with that drowsy softness that made Mr Charlton feel dreadfully congested, sweating, and messy, sure that she was mocking him. 'That's the way to be nice to anybody. First time.'

Unaware of it Mr Charlton said an extremely foolish thing:

'Aren't people always nice to you first time?'

'Depends.'

Mr Charlton, unaware of it again, said another foolish thing:

'Depends on what?'

She turned sideways, so that for the second time in his life Mr Charlton found himself confronted by an astral body of alarming shape, this time as firm and dark as ebony.

'On whether I let them.'

She had already started to peel the tissue paper from the orange lollipop when Mariette came in, carrying two baskets.

'Oh! company,' the girl said.

Peeling the last of the tissue paper from the orange lollipop,

94

she stared with flat cool eyes at Mariette. Mr Charlton thought Mariette's eyes looked, in reply, like two infuriated black bees.

'Well, I'll push off,' the girl said. 'See you later, Charley.' She tossed her hair from one side of her shoulders to another, at the same time giving Mr Charlton a glad, cool, backward look. 'If not before.'

She was hardly out of the tent before Mariette banged the two baskets on the table and shouted 'Tart!'

Mr Charlton was very much shaken.

'Steady,' he said. 'She'll hear –'

'She's meant to, the so-and-so, isn't she?'

'I really didn't want the thing,' Mr Charlton said. 'I told her to take it –'

'She'd take anything. She'd take the skin off your back – and a bit more if you let her!'

He had never seen Mariette angry before. Her voice sounded raw.

'She's nothing but a –' Mariette choked at some impossible word and then decided Mr Charlton wouldn't understand it. 'No, I won't say it. It's too good. I'll bottle it in. She's no virgin though!' she shouted, 'everybody knows that!'

Mr Charlton, who was not accustomed to hear the word virgin bandied about very much, especially in public, was relieved to see two more women approaching the tent, but was disappointed a moment later to see that they were Poll and Lil. He had made up his mind to remonstrate as tactfully as possible with Poll about rubbing out and altering the figures in the book from two to three and thus twisting him. He was convinced that that was what had happened.

But when he saw the two earringed women, one tall and scrawny as a scarecrow, the other brawny as a bare-armed fishwife, both as brown as gipsies, he suddenly lost heart and said to Mariette:

'Don't go for a minute. Stay until these two have gone. I want to talk to you –'

'I've got to cool off!' Mariette said. 'I'm going into the wood to cool off!'

'Wait just a minute –'

'I've got to cool off! That's where I'll be if you want me.'

A moment later he was alone with Poll and Lil, who had been having a conference as to whether they could twist him a second time so soon or whether they should leave it for a while and do a double twist next time. Between them they knew a few good ones and they generally worked better, for some funny reason, in the afternoon.

'Hullo, duckie,' they said. 'Here we are again.'

*

By the middle of the afternoon it was so hot that Mr Charlton got Montgomery and the twins to bring him a bucket of water drawn from a stand-pipe by the gate of the field. He drank a big draught or two of water and then plunged his head several times into the bucket and then dried his face on his handkerchief and combed his wet, cooled hair. After this he cleaned up his spectacles, polishing them on the driest piece of his shirt he could find, and went to stand at the door of the tent, slightly refreshed, to get a breath of air.

The sun hit the crown of his head like a brass cymbal. He had never known it so hot in May. It seemed to affect his eyesight for a moment and when he looked across the strawberry field he was astonished to see a startling change there.

Almost all the women had done what Poll and Lil had said they would do. They had stripped off their blouses and shirts in the heat and were working in nothing but bodices and brassieres. The effect was that the lines of coloured flags had now become like lines of white washing hung out in the blazing sun to dry.

Mr Charlton went back into the tent and tried to satisfy his curiosity about what Pop called the strawberry lark by adding up how many pounds of strawberries had been in and out of the tent that day. He calculated, astonishingly, that he had checked in more than a ton. That meant, he reasoned, a pretty fair lump for the pickers.

His trained mind wondered what the tax position about *that* was. He would have to ask Pop. He was sure Pop would know.

He was still thinking of this when he looked up and saw Pauline Jackson standing in the door. She was not wearing a black sweater now. Like the rest of the women she had stripped down to her brassiere. She had very fine sun-tanned arms and shoulders but the lower part of her deep chest was as white as the inside of a young apple by comparison.

It was this startling whiteness that made his heart start bouncing. She smiled. She came to the table and said in her lazy way:

'Not much cooler, is it?'

She put twenty-four pounds of strawberries on the table. He started to fumble with pencil and paper, his eyes downcast. She leaned forward as if to see what he was writing down and said:

'How many does that make for me today? Eight dozen?'

He started to say 'I've got an idea it's more than that, Miss Jackson,' determined to keep it as formal as possible, and then looked up to see, not ten or twelve inches from his face, most of her bared, white, perfectly sculptured bust, blazingly revealed, heaving deeply.

Like Ma, Miss Jackson did not seem unduly perturbed.

'Two more dozen,' she said, 'and I think I'll pack it up for the day.'

'I see. Are you paid every day, Miss Jackson, or do you leave it till the week-end?'

'What makes you keep calling me Miss Jackson?'

He started to write in the book again when she said:

'What time are you knocking off? Going back to Fordington? If you are I could give you a lift on my Vespa.'

Where on earth did these people get the money from? Mr Charlton started thinking. He supposed –

'What about it?' she said.

Too nervous to think clearly, Mr Charlton said:

'I don't know what time I'll finish. I did want to go to Fordington to fetch some clothes from my room, but –'

'Might go on and have a swim at the pool', she said, 'afterwards. How about that?'

He said: 'Well –'

'I could wait.' The sculptured breasts rose and fell heavily and came an inch or two nearer, their division so deep and the pure whiteness so sharp in the shade of the tent, against the dark brown upper flesh of her shoulders, that Mr Charlton was utterly mesmerized. 'No hurry for half an hour one way or the other. Just tell me when.'

She swung her body away. He saw the splendid curves turn full circle in such a way that he was dizzy in the heat. She laughed and reached the door as he stuttered:

'You know, I actually couldn't say if – I mean, there's nothing definite –'

'Just say when,' she said. 'All you got to do is to tell me when.'

She had hardly disappeared before Poll and Lil came in.

They too had stripped down to the bust and Poll had an un-lighted cigarette dangling from her lips. They had decided to work a new one on Mr Charlton.

'Hullo, duckie,' they said and Poll took the cigarette from her lips, broke it in half, and gave one half to Lil. 'Last one, dear. Not unless Charley can help us out. Haven't got a gasper, duckie, I suppose?'

Mr Charlton, who smoked moderately at the best of times, had recently given it up altogether because he was scared of cancer.

'Afraid not. Don't smoke now –'

'Came out without a bean this morning,' Poll explained. 'Too early for the damn Post Office. Else we'd have got the kids' allowances.'

'How many baskets?' Mr Charlton said.

'Three dozen.' Poll lit her cigarette and then gave Lil a light, both of them exhaling smoke in desperate relief. 'Gawd, it's hot out in that field. You want a drag every two minutes to keep you going at all. Don't suppose you could lend us five bob so's Lil can nip down to the shop on her bike, can you? Pay you back first thing tomorrow.'

Mr Charlton wrote desperately in the book while the two bare-chested women watched him, though he did not know it, like two brown, hungry, calculating old dogs watching a bone. There probably wasn't much meat on Mr Charlton; they'd better get it off while they could.

'Five bob, duckie. Gawd, it's hot out in that field. Two women fainted. Did you hear about that, duckie? Two women fainted.'

'Work it orf as dead horse,' Lil started to say.

Touched, nervous, and swayed against his better judgement, Mr Charlton was just thinking of lending Poll and Lil the five bob to be worked off as dead horse when he heard, from the field, a sudden pandemonium of yelling and shrieking.

He followed Poll and Lil to the door of the tent. Thirty yards from the tent a ring of semi-naked vultures were shrieking and flapping in the sun. 'Somebody's at it. Somebody's catching a packet,' Poll said and Mr Charlton caught a glimpse, somewhere in the vultured circle, of two bare-shouldered girls fighting each other, like wild white cats.

Poll and Lil started running. Mr Charlton started running too. Then, after ten yards or so, he suddenly stopped as if his head had been caught by an invisible trip-wire.

One of the white cats was Pauline Jackson; the other was Mariette. Like cats too they were howling in the unrestricted animal voices that belong to dark roof tops. With alarm Mr Charlton saw streams of blood on the flesh of hands, faces, bare shoulders, and half-bare breasts, and then suddenly realized that this was really the scarlet juice of smashed strawberries that the girls were viciously rubbing into each other's eyes and throat and hair. The fair horse-tail was like frayed red rope and the neat dark curls of Mariette that he cared for more and more every time he saw them were being torn from her face. Somewhere in the centre of it all the colossal bulk of Ma was shouting; but whether in encouragement, discouragement, or sheer delight he never knew.

Half a minute later he heard the highest shrieking of all. It came from behind him. He turned sharply and saw The Little Two-penn'orth running from the shelter of the wood, waving her tiny arms in excitement. That high-pitched voice of hers was more like a train-whistle than ever.

When she reached him she started bobbing wildly up and down, like a child too small to see over a fence, and Mr Charlton realized that she could not see any part of the cat-and-strawberry horror that by now had him completely spell-bound.

'Hold me up, mister!' she shrieked. 'I s'll miss it!'

He took her by the arms and the tiny body rose into the air like a spring.

'Blimey, it's good!' she shrieked. 'It's good!' By now she was actually sitting on Mr Charlton's shoulder, her tiny short legs drumming continually on his chest and her fists in his hair. 'That'll take some getting out in the wash. Git stuck into her, Mariette! It's good! It's good! It's good!'

Mr Charlton didn't think it was good. He was afraid Mariette would get seriously hurt and he felt a little sick at the thought of it. Suddenly he felt constrained to rush in and separate the two combatants, all scarlet now and weeping and half-naked, before they disfigured each other for ever; and he said:

'I've got to stop them. I've got to make them stop it. Any-way, what on earth are they fighting *for*?'

'Gawd Blimey, don't you *know*, mister?' The Little Two-penn'orth shrieked. 'Don't tell me you don't *know*!'

Even when he was riding home that evening in the back of the truck Mr Charlton still could not really believe that he knew. The notion that two girls would fight for him still had him completely stunned.

Everybody had been sternly briefed by Ma, before the truck arrived, not to say a word to Pop. 'Might give her a good leatherin' if he knew,' Ma explained, 'and it's hot enough as it is.'

Everybody agreed; they were all for Mariette. Mr Charlton was all for Mariette too; he felt himself grow continually more proud of her as the truck, driven at Pop's customary jolting speed, rocked homewards through fragrant hedgerows of honeysuckle, the first wild pink roses and may. He kept smiling at her and watching her dark, pretty, red-stained hair. Somebody had lent her a green sweater to wear over her ripped bodice and you could hardly tell, now, that she had been in a fight at all.

In a curious way it was Mr Charlton who felt he had been in a fight. A total lack of all feeling of uncertainty, together with an odd sensation of actual aggression, began to make him feel rather proud of himself too.

'Well, how was the first day, Charley?' Pop said. In the sitting-room Pop had poured out a Dragon's Blood for himself and one for Mr Charlton, who felt he really needed it. He was as hungry as a hunter too. 'How was the first day? Everything go orf all right? Smooth an' all that? No lumbago?'

'No lumbago,' Mr Charlton said. 'Everything smooth as it could be.'

'Perfick,' Pop said.

He drank Dragon's Blood to the day's perfection and called through to the kitchen to Ma:

'How long'll supper be, Ma? I'm turning over.'

'About an hour yet. Roast beef's only just gone in.'

'How'd you get on today, Ma? Good picking?'

'Earned fourteen pound ten,' Ma said.

'Hour yet,' Pop said to Mr Charlton, 'plenty o' time for you to take Mariette for a stroll as far as the river. They'll be cutting the grass in that medder tomorrow.'

Mr Charlton agreed; he had his thoughts very much on the buttercup field.

Just before going outside, however, he remembered that he had a question to ask of Pop. It was the one about tax on the strawberry lark.

'An awful lot of money gets paid out to these people,' he

said. 'Strawberries. Cherries. Hops and so on. Take for example all these Cockneys coming down for the hops. Strictly, in law, they ought to pay tax on that.'

'Pay tax?' Pop said. He spoke faintly.

'I mean if the law is to be interpreted in the strict letter –'

'Strick letter my aunt Fanny,' Pop said. 'Dammit if they was taxed they wouldn't come. Then you wouldn't have no strawberries, no cherries, no nothink. No beer!'

The logic of this argument dashed the last of Mr Charlton's reasoning and he went away to find Mariette, who was just coming downstairs, dressed now in the cool green shantung of which he had grown so very fond.

As Mr Charlton and Mariette disappeared across the yard in the evening sun Ma's only complaint, as she watched them from the kitchen window, was that she hadn't got a pair of field-glasses, so that she could watch 'how that young man's getting on with his technique. If he's getting on at all'.

Pop, after pouring two gills of gin into his second Dragon's Blood in order to pep it up a bit, retired to watch television. It had been on for some considerable time, out of natural habit, though no one was watching it, and now there was a programme on the screen about life in central Africa, about wild animals, pygmies, and their strange, baffling customs.

Pop sat back happily in the greenish unreal semi-darkness. He had had a very good day doing a big lark in scrap that showed six hundred per cent with not a very great deal of trouble. He would tell Ma all about it later. Meanwhile he was perfectly content to sit and sip his beer and watch the pygmies, all of whom hopped about the jungle and the village compounds with unconcern, without a stitch on, all the women bare-breasted. There was hardly a programme he liked better than those about strange hot countries, wild animals, and queer tribes, especially those who had never seen civilization.

Out in the buttercup field Mariette and Mr Charlton were lying in the tall brilliant flowers and the even taller feathery grasses. Mariette, so dark and so pretty in her green shantung, was drawing Mr Charlton very gently to her and Mr Charlton was responding with a proud, searching look on his face so that Ma, if she could have been watching him at that moment through binoculars, would have seen that he had gone some way, in certain directions, towards improving his technique.

6

WHEN Pop got home the following evening he found Miss Pilchester waiting in the yard.

'Isn't it absolutely ghastly?' Miss Pilchester said.

The evening seemed warmer than ever, but Miss Pilchester was wearing a thick thorn-proof skirt of cabbage green and a cable-stitch woollen cardigan to match. Pop did not ask her what was absolutely ghastly and she did not offer to tell him either.

There was no need. Everything to Edith Pilchester was always absolutely ghastly. She lived alone and kept numbers of laying hens. The hens were absolutely ghastly, and so, even worse, was living alone. It was absolutely impossible to get any help in the house, in the garden, or with the hens. She couldn't afford to run a car because of taxes and the price of petrol and oil and servicing and repairs. She could just afford a solitary hack of her own, but she couldn't afford a groom. It was all absolutely ghastly. Before the war she had kept a little maid in the house, a man in the garden, and a groom-cum-chauffeur-cum-cook who was an absolute treasure in all sorts of ways, including bringing her early morning tea and hot whisky last thing at night in bed. Now all of them had gone and she could hardly afford the whisky. It was absolutely ghastly. Everybody went out to work in the fields at strawberry-picking, cherry-picking, plum-picking, apple-picking, bean-picking, hop-picking, or at the canning-factories in the town, earning mountains more money than they knew what to do with and in any case more than she could pay. It was all absolutely ghastly.

One of the results of everything being so absolutely ghastly was that Miss Pilchester, who was a fortyish, slightly-moustached brunette shaped like a bolster, threw herself into an amazing number of projects with an energy quite ferocious, desperately trying to put the whole ghastly business to rights again. Prowling from committee to committee, charity to charity, bazaar to bazaar, she was like some restless, thirsty lioness seeking prey.

'Hot again, ain't it?' Pop said.

'Absolutely ghastly.'

When Pop suggested that Miss Pilchester should come into the house and have a drink and cool off a bit Miss Pilchester said no thanks, not for the moment, it was absolutely ghastly. She thought they ought to do the field; there wasn't much time left, thanks to that bounder Fortescue letting them down at the last moment and the committee, with the exception of the Brigadier, having been very nearly as bad. The whole thing was simply too ghastly.

Over in the meadow the grass had been cut and baled during the day. Big fragrant cotton-reels of hay lay scattered everywhere between the house and the river. Only a white and yellow fringe of moon-daisy and buttercup remained standing at the edges, pretty as a ruffle under the hedgerows of hawthorn, rising honeysuckle, and wild rose.

'Damn good field, Larkin,' Miss Pilchester said. 'No doubt about that. Just the job.'

She surveyed it with critical, organizing eye, seeing on it a vision of jumps, judges' tents, show-rings, beer-tents, and horses. It was awfully decent of Larkin to do it, she said, otherwise everything would have been an absolute shambles.

'Always like to oblige,' Pop said and laughed in cheerful fashion.

Miss Pilchester laughed too. One of the things she always liked about Larkin was the man's inexhaustible cheerfulness. Friendly chap.

'What about the car-park though?' she said. 'That's always another nightmare.'

'Use the other field,' Pop said. 'Next door. The little 'un. Simple.'

Swallows were flying high above the meadows and the river, swooping in the blue hot sky, and Miss Pilchester might almost have been one of them in the quick, darting glances of gratitude she gave to Pop.

'All yours,' Pop said. 'Come and go just as you like. Any time.'

Another thing Miss Pilchester liked about Pop was the terrific easy generosity of the chap. Good sport. She had once been casually kissed by Pop at a Christmas village social, in some game or other, and the experience, for her at least, had been something more than that of two pairs of lips briefly meeting. It gave you the same feeling, she thought, as smelling bruised spring grass, or new-mown hay, for the first time.

'All we want then is a fine day,' Miss Pilchester said. 'If it's wet it'll be absolutely ghastly.'

'Can't control the tap-water I'm afraid,' Pop said and laughed again, at the same time remarking how thirsty he was. 'Might put something in it, though, if you feel like it now. Drop o' gin? Drop o' whisky? Glass o' port?'

Miss Pilchester darted towards Pop another rapid, swallow-like glance of approval, half-affectionate, half-grateful, her eyes so momentarily absorbed in the baldish, perky profile with its dark side-linings that she quite forgot to say that anything was absolutely ghastly.

Back in the yard a van from the bacon factory had just

delivered all of Pop's two pigs – he had decided after all that one would be gone almost before you could wink – except the four sides and two hams, which had been left for curing. In the kitchen, Ma, now a white-aproned expansive butcheress, was busy trimming several score pounds of pork and pork-offal; cheerful as ever she stowed it away in the new deep-freeze. As Pop put his head through the kitchen door he was confronted by a bloodstained mountain of legs, loins, heads, chitterlings, and trotters and the sight gave him enormous pleasure. Ma said:

'Dr Leagrave's in the sitting-room. I said you wouldn't be long.'

'Come to see Mariette?'

'No, pipe down, you loony. Nobody knows anything about that. No: just on his way back from the golf-course. Just passing.'

'Thirsty, I expect,' Pop said. 'Still, just the job – we can get him to run the rule over Mister Charlton.'

In the sitting-room Pop introduced Miss Pilchester to Dr Leagrave, who was a heavyish man in his fifties, rather red-necked in a Teutonic sort of way, and completely bald. The doctor, who played a good deal of golf as a pretence of getting exercise and keeping his weight down, though in reality pre-ferring the comforts of the club-house, remarked that it was warmish. Miss Pilchester said it was absolutely ghastly and flopped into an easy chair with the grace of a cow.

Television was on, out of natural habit, and the programme was one of opera, the composer being a man named Wagner, of whom Pop had never heard. Pop gave the screen a cursory, whipping glance – the programmes were never much catch Tuesdays – and wondered if everybody on it had gone stark, staring mad.

It was a relief to turn to drinks and Miss Pilchester:

'Now, Miss Pilchester. Edith.' Miss Pilchester bloomed softly, smiling as Pop called her Edith. 'What shall it be? Drop o' whisky? Drop o' gin? Drop o' Guinness? I can make you a cocktail.'

Miss Pilchester said she thought cocktails were absolutely ghastly. 'No, whisky for me. And soda please.'

Dr Leagrave chose the same. Pop, in brief thought over the cocktail galleon, wondered if he should mix himself a real snorter, such as a Rolls-Royce or a Chauffeur, but finally decided to have his favourite Dragon's Blood with lime.

'Your day off, doc?' he said.

Dr Leagrave thanked God it was and took his whisky with uncertain but eager hands.

'It must be absolutely ghastly in this heat,' Miss Pilchester said, 'sick-visiting and all that.'

'Not that so much,' the doctor said. 'Trouble is it's a nice fine evening. By now my waiting-room'll be as jam-packed as a cinema with Lolla showing.'

Sipping whisky, an astonished Miss Pilchester asked why that should be and got the answer not from Dr Leagrave, but from Pop, himself as quick as a swallow:

'Ain't got nothing better to do. That's why.'

'Hit it plumb on the head,' the doctor said.

'You mean it makes a difference?' Miss Pilchester said, 'what the weather is?'

'More perfick the wevver,' Pop said, 'the more they roll up. You told me that once afore, didn't you, doc?'

The doctor said indeed he had.

'Absolutely ghastly,' Miss Pilchester said.

'Fast becoming a nation of hypochondriacs,' the doctor said, and Pop looked so suddenly startled at yet another word he had never even heard on television that he couldn't speak. That was the second within a few days. 'Pill-takers. Drug-takers.'

'Ghastly.'

'Then there are young doctors,' Dr Leagrave said, now launching on a tried and favourite theme, 'men of not very great experience, who are prescribing a hundred, two hundred, capsules of new and highly expensive drugs to patients who take two and put the rest into the kitchen cupboard.'

'Ghastly.'

With something like venom Dr Leagrave finished his whisky, his seventh since six o'clock, and said it was no wonder the country was on its beam-ends. Miss Pilchester warmly agreed and Pop took away the doctor's empty glass to fill it up again, at the same time glancing at the television screen, unable to make any sense whatever of a single note or gesture coming out of it.

As soon as he had poured the doctor's whisky he decided to switch the sound off. He couldn't bear to switch the picture off in case something should come on, like pygmies or football or chorus girls, which he liked. In consequence the screen became a pallid mime of open-mouthed puppets singing silently.

'By the way, doc,' he said, 'we got a young friend of ours staying here who's bad a-bed and wuss up. Think you could have a look at him?'

'What's wrong?' the doctor said. 'Not another pill-addict, I hope.'

'Lumbago,' Pop said.

'Ghastly,' Miss Pilchester said. 'I get it. I sympathize.'

Pop said he would try to find Mr Charlton and started to go out of the room, remembering as he did so the kitchen piled with pork.

'Nice piece o' pork for you when you go, doc,' he said. 'How about that? You too, Edith. Like chitterlings?' Pop laughed in his infectious, rousing fashion. 'How about a nice piece o' pig's liver and a basin o' chitterlings?'

Miss Pilchester, who had not yet been reduced to eating chitterlings, nevertheless laughed too. Always made you feel happy, that man, she thought. When Pop came back with a rather hesitant but sun-scorched Mr Charlton, red-faced from a second day in the strawberry fields and more ravenously hungry than he had ever been in his life, the doctor was just saying to Edith Pilchester, again with a sort of evangelical, venomous uncertainty:

'This county alone is spending over a million a year on drugs! This one county –'

'Here's our young friend,' Pop said. 'Friend of Mariette's. Mister Charlton. Been very poorly.'

'Well,' the doctor said, 'perhaps we can have a look at you.' He glanced uncertainly round at Miss Pilchester. 'Is there somewhere –'

'Upstairs,' Pop said. 'I'll lead the way.'

Mr Charlton followed Pop and Dr Leagrave upstairs. On the landing Pop paused to whisper confidentially to the doctor that there would be a whole leg of pork if he wanted it; he hadn't very well been able to say it in front of Edith – the doc would understand?

The doctor, swaying a little, said he understood, and Pop opened the first door on the landing without knocking.

'This'll do,' he said. 'Mariette's room.'

Fortunately the room was empty and presently Mr Charlton, stripped to the waist, found himself lying face downwards on Mariette's bed, his sensations very like those he had experienced when the geese had entwined their necks about his legs, when he had worn Mariette's pyjamas and when, in utter ecstasy, he had breathed the fragrance of gardenia for the first time. The hot room was thick and intoxicating with that same deep, torturing fragrance now.

The doctor, who had not bothered to fetch his bag from the car, pressed his fingers gently into Mr Charlton's lumbar region.

'Much pain?'

Mr Charlton confessed that he had no pain whatever. A day in the strawberry fields had in fact improved him so much, both physically and mentally, that he had actually spotted the double twist Poll and Lil were going to work on him almost before they had started.

'Comes and goes? That it?'

'Sort of like that.'

'Suppose you'd like to go on sick benefit for a couple of weeks?'

To the doctor's astonishment Mr Charlton said no, he didn't think so. He was, though he didn't say so, having a wonderful time in the strawberry field. He was earning money. If he went on sick benefit he wouldn't earn any money and he wouldn't have half the fun. He was learning to use his loaf.

'Well,' the doctor said, 'try to keep out of draughts when you're hot.' He laughed briefly, swayed tipsily, and thought of how perhaps it would be possible to snatch another quick one downstairs before he took the leg of pork and went home. 'And avoid lying in wet grasses.'

Some time after the doctor had gone Pop wrapped up two pounds of loin of pork, about a pound of liver, and a pair of pig's trotters and said that, if Edith was ready, he would run her home. Edith Pilchester, charmed with three whiskies, more than she usually had in a week, and enough food to last her until Sunday, was more than ready and completely forgot, for the second time, to say how absolutely ghastly anything was.

'Got a Rolls now,' Pop said.

Miss Pilchester confessed she had seen it in the yard.

'I said to myself it couldn't be yours.'

In the yard, Pop spent some time, with touches of imperial pride, showing Miss Pilchester the Rolls's burnished monograms, the silver vases for flowers, and the speaking tube.

'If you'd like to sit in the back,' he said, 'you can say things down the tube to me. Orders and all that.'

'I don't want to sit in the back,' Miss Pilchester said. 'Not on your life. I want to sit in the front with you.'

As they drove along Pop demonstrated first the town horn, the sweet one, then the country, the snarl. Miss Pilchester enjoyed this but said, 'Not so fast. I don't like driving so fast,' remembering that she lived less than a mile away. Accordingly Pop slowed down, driving with one hand and with the other half-caressing, half-pinching Miss Pilchester's knee. Since she wore only loose lisle stockings this, he found, was not half so delicious an experience as pinching Ma, who wore nylons and very tight ones at that, but to Miss Pilchester it seemed to be a source of palpitating pleasure.

She again became like a swallow, darting nervous, rapid glances.

A few minutes later the Rolls drew up at Bonny Banks, Miss Pilchester's cottage, tiny, thatched, and low-pitched, which she had converted out of a fallen down cow-byre in pre-war days, when things were cheap. Creosoted beams and a gimcrack front door studded with what appeared to be rusty horse-shoe nails were designed to give the little loaf-shaped house an appearance of Tudor antiquity or of having come out of a fairy-tale. But in the evening light, after the hot day, its garden ill-kept, the lawn unmown, the paths a flourish of dandelions, the rose-beds pitted with dust-baths made by escaping hens, it looked shabby even by comparison with Pop's paradise.

Miss Pilchester begged Pop over and over again not to look at it. It was simply ghastly, absolutely ghastly.

'You'll come in for a moment though, won't you?'

Pop had always wanted to see the inside of Miss Pilchester's cottage but when he groped his way through the kitchen, which smelt stale from unwashed dishes, and into a living-room as dark and cramped as a bolt-hole, even he was surprised. A flock of sheep might well have passed through the place an hour before. Bits of wool – raw, unwashed sheep's wool – lay everywhere. It was one of Miss Pilchester's hobbies to gather wool from field and hedgerow and on long winter's nights clean, spin, and wind it for making into socks and jumpers, which she dyed in subdued rough shades with lichen.

'Do take a pew if you can find room, won't you?'

It was difficult, if not impossible, to find a pew. Miss Pilchester hastily removed a basin of eggs, a half-finished jumper, two skeins of wool, *The Times*, a sewing-basket, some grey underwear, and an unplucked brown fowl from various chairs.

'Sit you down. I'll have a drink for you in a jiff. Don't mind anything. I'll just find a plate for the pork and then get some glasses.'

Remains of a boiled egg, a cup of cocoa, and a burnt raspberry tart, the left-overs either of breakfast or lunch, or both, lay scattered about the table. Miss Pilchester gathered up egg and cocoa, dropped the shell into the cocoa and then upset the resulting mess into the raspberry tart.

Some seconds later she was calling from the kitchen:

'Absolutely ghastly having no help. But nobody does, do they? Only Professor Fane.'

Fane, a professor of physics, with some distinguished degrees, including foreign ones, used the house next door as a week-end cottage only, coming down on Friday evenings to be bullied for three whole days by an ex-naval artificer and his wife, acting as chauffeur and cook, who borrowed the car all day on Sundays to visit other naval men by the sea or watch dirt-track racing on the hills. The professor spent most of the time in a ten-by-six attic under the roof, listening to Bach and Beethoven, while the ex-artificer and his wife used the drawing-room downstairs watching the television set that the professor had had to install in order to get them to stay in the house at all.

'He's lucky,' Miss Pilchester called. 'I can't get a soul.'

She was looking in various cupboards for a bottle of whisky, which she knew was there. It wasn't there and it was some moments before she found it tucked away behind another pile of underclothes, a basket of clothes pegs, and a vegetable marrow left over from last year.

An inch of whisky lay in the bottom and Miss Pilchester remembered she had not bought another bottle since she had had a cold at Easter, over six weeks before.

She put another inch of tap water into the bottle and then poured the whisky and water into two glasses, and calling, 'Just coming. Sorry I kept you so long,' went out of the kitchen to find Pop glancing at *The Times*, a newspaper he had never heard of before.

'No television?' Pop said.

'Couldn't possibly afford it.'

'Terrible,' Pop said.

With sudden irritation Miss Pilchester remembered some stock exchange figures she had been reading at breakfast and found herself in half a mind to ask Pop what he thought she ought to do with her $3\frac{1}{2}\%$ War Stock. He seemed so clever about money. He must be. The stock was another government swindle. She had bought it at ninety-six, and now it stood at sixty-seven – that was the way they treated you for being prudent, thrifty, and careful.

It was perfectly true, as someone or other had remarked to her only the other day, that all governments were dishonest.

'Don't you think all governments are dishonest?' she said. She handed Pop the whisky and explained about the shares. 'All they think about is getting out of you the little you've got. What do you think?'

'What do I think?' Pop said. 'I think you want to get it out o' *them* afore they have a chance to get it out o' *you.*'

Miss Pilchester laughed. She said 'Cheers' and, drinking an economical sip of whisky, thanked Pop once again for being so nice about the field.

'Going to pay your Hunt subscription next season? Hope so.'

Pop said of course he was going to pay a subscription; and one for Mariette too.

'Thank the Good God there are a few chaps like you.'

The Hunt, Miss Pilchester said, was going down. Hardly anybody had any time. The Christmas Meet last year had been an absolute rag-tag-and-bobtail. It was simply ghastly.

'Captain Prettyman's retiring as Master next year,' she said and thanked the Good God a second time. 'Never has been any good. Never got hold of the right end of the stick from the beginning.'

She darted Pop another of her rapid, swallow-like glances.

'You're the sort of chap they ought to have. New blood to pep them up.'

Pop could hardly bear it. In an uncertain spasm of ambition he actually had a swift vision of himself as Master of Fox Hounds. It was dazzling. At the present time he paid a sub-scription but never rode to hounds, though Mariette always did. The incredible idea of his being Master had never once occurred to him.

'Here, steady on, old girl,' he said. 'You'll get me started thinking things.'

Miss Pilchester, remembering the brief interlude when Pop had pressed her knee in the car, laughed as softly as she could.

'Well, that's always nice, isn't it?' she said.

Suddenly Pop did the thing Miss Pilchester feared most: he drained his whisky in a single gulp, smacking his lips with pleasure, as if ready to go. There was no more whisky left, not even a drop to water down, and she experienced a second of panic before he got up from the chair.

'Well, I must push back. Got a few things to do before bed-time.'

'Oh! must you go?'

With uncertainty Miss Pilchester got up too. She had been careful to sit with her back to the little cottage window, but now twilight was falling rapidly enough to make it almost impossible to distinguish the smaller details of her face. Only her eyes were bright as they gave Pop yet another quick, swallow-like dart.

'You've been an absolute lamb,' she said. 'Don't know how –'

She turned suddenly to find herself wrapped in Pop Larkin's arms, being kissed in splendid silence, with something of the effect of a velvet battering ram. This was the way Pop always kissed Ma but Miss Pilchester, for her part, had never experienced anything quite like it. It had on her something of the effect of Pop's cocktail on Mr Charlton: it explored with disquieting fire a few corners of her body that she hardly knew existed before.

When it was over Pop retired a few inches, took breath and said, in almost exactly the tones he always used when mixing drinks at the glittering Spanish galleon:

'How about one more?'

'Please.'

'Perfick,' Pop said.

Five minutes later a palpitating but very happy Miss Pilchester, trebly kissed – one more for luck, Pop had said – came to the gate of the little garden wilderness to wave him goodbye. If it had been possible she would have kissed him goodbye but she knew that even in the gathering May twilight the ex-artificer's wife would be watching from a window. Not that she cared a damn now. She felt dedicated for ever, with abandon, to the generous, passionate Mr Larkin.

'See you soon!' she waved.

'Any time,' Pop said. He laughed merrily. 'Don't do anything I wouldn't do. Keep your hand on your ha'penny.'

The last of Miss Pilchester's darting glances, this one almost of fire, seemed actually to set the Rolls in motion and with a neat, side-long wink he drove away.

At first he drove rather fast and then, suddenly subdued by the immensely incredible notion that he might one day become Master of Fox Hounds, slowed down to a silent crawl. He didn't want anybody to think he was drunk in charge. Two minutes later he passed a policeman on duty. Seeing the Rolls, the policeman saluted. Pop saluted in reply.

He'd have to tell Ma, he thought, about the Master of Fox

Hounds lark. No, he wouldn't though. He'd keep that after all; she'd say he was flying too high. What he would tell her, though, was about the inside of Miss Pilchester's house; that terrible, cramped, untidy, woolly, television-less little bolt-hole. Perfickly awful how some people lived, he would tell Ma, perfickly awful.

When he arrived home Ma was sitting outside the kitchen door, enjoying a Guinness and a few potato crisps after her battle with the pork. It was still hot in the semi-darkness, but Pop feared he could hear, in the distance, a few muted notes of thunder.

'Where's Mr Charlton?' he said.

'Been writing letters,' Ma said. 'Just gone off with Mariette to post them.'

'*Writing letters?*'

Another high, incredible mark of credit for Mr Charlton.

'Whatever's he got to write letters for?'

Impossible to understand how anybody could write letters.

'I think he'd been writing to the tax office.'

'Not about us,' Pop said. 'He ain't got nothing to write there about us.'

'Oh! no,' Ma said. Enjoying her Guinness, she was quite unperturbed. 'I think he's gone and extended his sick-leave. That's all. Since he saw the doctor. Going to stay another week or two.'

'Perfick,' Pop said. 'Jolly good.'

Pop, for whom Mr Charlton was rapidly becoming a more and more agreeable figure, quite exceptional in his literacy, went into the house to pour himself a Dragon's Blood. When he came back Ma said:

'Well, did you kiss her?'

'Course I did.'

'I thought you would.' Ma sat with the Guinness balanced on the precipice of her rolling stomach like a little black doll, again completely unperturbed. 'Do her good. Make her sleep all the sweeter. What was it like?'

Pop considered. He remembered how, in the twilight, some portion of Miss Pilchester's moustache had brushed against him.

'A bit like trying to catch a mole', he said, 'in a dark entry.'

Ma dug him sharply in the ribs and started laughing like a jelly. Pop laughed too at his own joke and then stared up at the sky, his attention rapt for some moments by the young, unquenchable summer stars. A few drops of rain fell, as if by a miracle, from a cloudless heaven, and then ceased in a whisper. Laughing made Pop give a sudden belch and far away, across miles of windless fields, somewhere on the dim hills, nature echoed him in a scarcely audible double note of thunder. Ma looked at the stars too and Pop started to tell her, true amazement in his voice, about Miss Pilchester's little Tudor bolt-hole and how perfickly awful it was.

'Never credit it, Ma,' he told her. 'Never credit it. Still, what I always say: you don't know, do you, until you get a look inside?'

For a few moments longer they sat in silence, until at last Ma said:

'Well: I'm waiting.'

'What for?'

'Don't you think it's about time you kissed *me*?'

Pop said he supposed it was. He drained his Dragon's Blood and set the empty glass behind his chair. Then he leaned over and clasped in his right hand as much of Ma's vast bosom as he could hold.

'It's coming to something', Ma said, 'when I have to ask you for one. Are you tired?'

Pop demonstrated that he was far from tired by kissing Ma with prolonged velvety artistry. Ma responded by settling back into her chair into a cocoon of silence unbroken except for an occasional exquisite breath of pleasure, exactly like the murmur of a kitten in a doze.

In the far distance new waves of thunder rolled. From the cloudless heaven a few fresh warm drops of rain fell. For some moments they splashed the two faces as lightly as a sigh but Pop and Ma, like the youngest of lovers, did not heed them at all.

7

ON the day of the pony gymkhana Mr Charlton was up at half past four. The morning was humid, dreamy, and overcast, with low mist on the river. Pop, who had already been up an hour, giving swill to pigs and fodder to the Jersey cow, and was now staunching back the first pangs of hunger with a few slices of bread and Cheddar cheese doused half an inch thick with tomato-ketchup, said he thought 'the wevver looked a little bit thick in the clear' but otherwise, with luck, it ought to be all right by noon.

Mr Charlton breakfasted on two lean pork cutlets, some scrambled eggs cooked by Mariette, fried potatoes, and four halves of tomato.

'In the old days,' said Pop, whose estimation of Mr Charlton rose almost every time he talked to him, especially on occasions like coming down to breakfast at a good time and getting outside a reasonable amount of food, 'my Dad used to tell me that they always had beer for breakfast. Like a glass o' beer?'

Mr Charlton thanked him and said he didn't think he would. Mariette had just made tea.

'Well, I think I will,' Pop said. 'I don't think a lot o' tea is all that good for you.'

Pop, after pouring himself a Dragon's Blood, had much the same breakfast as Mr Charlton, except that there was a lot more of it and that his plate was gay with mustard, ketchup, and two kinds of Worcester sauce. Mariette, who looked pretty and fresh in dark green slacks and a pale yellow shirt blouse, said she was so excited she could hardly eat but nevertheless managed two eggs and bacon, a pint of milk, and four slices of bread.

Ma was not yet down but had sent word that as the day was going to be a long one she was having a lay-in, which meant she would be down by half past six.

Towards the end of breakfast Pop turned to Mr Charlton, who had not been able to keep his eyes off Mariette for more than two seconds since she had come into the kitchen tying up her hair with a thin emerald ribbon, and said:

'Are you two going to feed and water the donkeys? I've got forty thousand jobs to do and Miss Pilchester'll be here by six.'

Mr Charlton said of course they would feed the donkeys and helped himself to a fifth slice of bread and covered it half an inch thick with fresh Jersey butter made by Ma. Pop watched this process with immense admiration, telling himself he had never seen such a change in a man's health as he had witnessed in three weeks in Mr Charlton.

Mr Charlton was still on sick leave.

'Oh! those sweet donkeys,' Mariette said.

The donkeys that she and Mr Charlton were going to feed were not the rest of the Larkin household but four animals Pop had secured for racing. Pop thought that gymkhanas were sometimes inclined to be on the dull side, what he called 'a bit horseface like – so many folks with long faces you can't very often tell the mares from some of the old women' – and that therefore something was needed to enliven the customary round of trotting, riding, leading rein, jumping, bending, and walk, trot, canter, and run.

This was why he had thought of the donkeys and why, later on in the day, he thought of introducing a few private harmless jokes of his own. What these were he was keeping to himself; but he had not forgotten the one about putting a firework under Miss Pilchester.

To his grievous disappointment the committee had turned down his offer of fireworks. It might well be, they had pointed out, that a few ponies would be late leaving the ground and that some fireworks would in any case go off early and the ponies be distressed. Pop saw the reason in this but if there was going to be one firework and only one it was, he was determined, going to be Miss Pilchester's.

'What time is the cocktail party, Pop?' Mr Charlton said.

Pop was delighted that Mr Charlton now called him Pop.

'Ma thinks eight o'clock would be the perfick time.'

'What a day,' Mariette said. 'All this and cocktails too.'

She went on to confess that she had never been to a cocktail party and Pop said:

'Come to that neither have I. Neither has Ma.'

'What do people normally drink at cocktail parties?' Mariette said.

'Cocktails,' Mr Charlton said slyly and before he could move she gave him a swift playful cuff, exactly like that of a dark soft kitten, across the head.

'Not at this one you don't,' Pop said.

Both Mariette and Mr Charlton were too excited to remember that the whole question of what was drunk at cocktail parties had been discussed a week before.

Since Pop had been unable to indulge himself with fireworks he and Ma had decided that there must, if possible, be something in their place. A cocktail party, Pop said, would be the perfick answer. Ma agreed, but said they ought to keep it very select if possible. Not more than thirty people, she thought, at the outside: mostly the committee and their families and of course nice people like the Miss Barnwells and the Luffingtons and the Brigadier. And what about eats?

Neither Pop nor Ma had any idea what you ate at cocktail parties; therefore Mr Charlton was consulted.

'Canapés, vol-au-vents, pistachios, and that sort of thing,' Mr Charlton said.

A lot more marks for Mr Charlton, Pop thought, as once again he heard words he had never even heard on television.

'You mean nuts and things?' Ma said. 'They won't keep anybody alive very long. I'd better cook a ham.'

Pop warmly agreed; the ham was firmly decided upon. Ma could cut plenty of the thinnest white and brown sandwiches, with nice Jersey butter. And what else?

Mariette said she thought small pieces of cold sardine on toast would be nice. 'They're absolutely marvellous hot too,' Mr Charlton said and got himself still more marks by also suggesting small squares of toast with hot Welsh rarebit, chicken sandwiches, and little sausages on sticks.

Most of this, to Pop, seemed rather light, unsatisfying fare.

'We want to give 'em enough,' he said. 'We don't want 'em to think we're starving 'em. What about a leg o' pork?'

To his disappointment Mr Charlton said he rather ruled out the leg of pork.

'All right,' Pop said. 'What about drinks?'

Pop was all for making plenty of Rolls-Royces and that sort of thing, good, strong ones, together with two new ones he had recently tried out from *The Guide to Better Drinking*: Red Bull and Ma Chérie. Red Bull was a blinder. That would curl their hair.

Mr Charlton said he thought it made it so much simpler if you stuck to two, or at the outside, three good drinks: say sherry, port, and gin-and-french. He suggested the port in case the evening was cool.

He got no marks this time. Pop thought it was all about as dull as flippin' ditchwater. With sudden enthusiasm he said:

'What about champagne?'

Both Ma and Mariette said they adored champagne. That was a brilliant idea. Something extra nice always happened, Mariette said, when you had champagne, and it seemed to Pop that he saw her exchange with Mr Charlton an intimate glance of secret tenderness that left him baffled and unsatisfied. Couldn't be nothing in the wind?

'Well, champagne it is then!' Pop said. 'Might as well do the thing properly.'

Here Mr Charlton remarked with tact that since not everybody liked champagne it might be just as well to have some other drink in reserve.

'I'll make a few hair-curlers,' Pop said. 'Red Bull – remember that one? – and Ma Chérie.'

Mr Charlton remembered Red Bull. It had rammed him one evening after a hardish day in the strawberry field. It was not inaptly named.

It was half past five before Mr Charlton and Mariette got up at last from breakfast and went across the yard to feed the donkeys. The four little donkeys had been tied up in the stable that Pop had built with his eye on the day when all the family, with the possible exception of Ma, would have a pony or a horse to ride. That would be the day. Two donkeys had been hired by Pop; two had been brought over by their owners the previous night. Three more, it was hoped, were still to come.

As soon as Mariette and himself were in the half-dark stable, among the donkeys, Mr Charlton took her quickly in his arms and kissed her. His arms and hands, as they tenderly touched her face, breasts, and shoulders, were as brown as her own.

Mariette laughed, trembling, and said she'd hardly been able to wait for that one, the first, the loveliest of the day. Mr Charlton, with something like ecstasy, said he hadn't been able to wait either. He could hardly wait for anything. Above all he could hardly wait for the afternoon. 'Nor me,' Mariette said and held her body out to him again.

Quietly, as the second kiss went on, the donkeys stirred about the stable, swishing tails, restless. Hearing them, Mariette partly broke away from Mr Charlton and said with half-laughing mouth:

'I suppose there's a first time for everything. I've never been kissed among donkeys before.'

Quick as a swallow himself, Mr Charlton answered. It was the answer of a man sharpened by three weeks in the strawberry field, living with the Larkins, and using his loaf.

'Wait till the cocktail party,' he said.

*

It was almost half past ten before Miss Pilchester fell bodily out of the taxi she had hired in desperation, four hours late, to bring her to the meadow. Pop, who was helping the Brigadier to string up gay lines of square and triangular flags about and among the tents, stared in stupefaction at a figure that might have been that of a tired and collapsing mountaineer descending from a peak. Miss Pilchester was armed with shooting stick, rolled mackintosh, a leather hold-all containing a spare cardigan, her lunch and a red vacuum flask, an attaché case containing the judging lists, *The Times*, several books, and a basket of pot-eggs. The pot-eggs, evidently brought for use in some pony event or other, rolled about the squatting Miss Pilchester exactly as if, in a sudden over-spasm of broodiness, she had laid them all herself.

It was all absolutely ghastly, but both Pop and the Brigadier were too stupefied to go over and pick up either Miss Pilchester or the eggs; and Pop, for once, was utterly without words. It was the Brigadier who spoke for him.

'Good God, Larkin,' he said, 'Edith must be either tight or egg-bound.'

Five minutes later Miss Pilchester, the great organizer, was at her work. This was all done, as the Brigadier himself pointed out, at a half canter. With indecisive excitement Miss Pilchester rushed from tent to tent, inquiring if someone had seen this, somebody that, had the caterers arrived, and above all wasn't it ghastly?

The caterers had been on the field since seven o'clock; all of them had knocked off for tea. Where, then, was the loud-speaker for announcements? Hadn't that arrived? It had arrived and Miss Pilchester tripped over two lines of its wires. Cancelled entries – were there any cancelled entries? – all entries, she wailed, should have been cancelled by nine o'clock.

It was now, the Brigadier was heard to point out dryly, half past ten.

Where then, Miss Pilchester wanted to know, were the donkeys? Were the donkeys here?

'Some donkeys', the Brigadier was heard to remark, 'have been here all night,' but the remark was lost on Miss Pilchester, who rushed away to inquire if the ladies' conveniences had been installed. 'They are most important,' she said and disappeared into a far tent as if feeling it suddenly necessary to prove it for herself.

At half past eleven the sun broke through, beginning to dry

at last the heavy dew on the grass, the trees of the bluebell wood, and the hedgerows. From the completely windless river the last transparent breaths of mist began to rise. A few water-lilies were in bud, heads rising above wet leaves, and they looked like pipes, gently smoking.

It was then discovered that Miss Pilchester had completely forgotten to meet a London train, as she had faithfully promised, at ten forty-five. The train was bringing a judge who had, in counties west of London, a great reputation for judging such things as The Horse of the Year Show. The committee had specially asked for him.

Now Ma came hurrying from the house to say she'd had a bulldog on the phone. 'And *did* he bark. And *oh!* the language.'

'Why the 'ell couldn't he come by car?' Pop said.

'Said he flipping well couldn't afford one under this flipping government.'

'*We must do something!*' Miss Pilchester said. 'It's absolutely ghastly!'

'Mariette and Mr Charlton can fetch him in the station-wagon,' Pop said. 'They've got to collect more champagne anyway. Ma don't think we've got enough.'

'Champagne? What champagne? Who ordered champagne?'

'I did.'

'*Not for this show?*'

'Cocktail party,' Pop said. 'Me and Ma. Instead of the fireworks tonight. You got your invite, didn't you? Mariette and Mr Charlton sent all the invites out.'

The word fireworks dragged Miss Pilchester back to Pop's side like a struggling dog on a lead.

'Now you will promise, won't you, no fireworks?'

'No fireworks,' Pop said.

Miss Pilchester, remembering Pop's delicate investigation of her knee in the Rolls, the velvety battering ram of the kiss that, as Ma had predicted, had made her sleep so much more sweetly, now permitted herself the luxury of a half-smile, the first of her hurried day.

'I know you. Sometimes you're more than naughty.'

Sun twinkled on Pop's eyes, lighting up the pupils in a face that otherwise remained as dead as a dummy.

'Not today though,' Pop said. 'Got to behave today.'

'And promise no fireworks?'

'No fireworks.'

'Not one?'

'Not one,' Pop said and fixed his eyes on the hem of her skirt as she rushed away to attend once again to the matter of the ladies' conveniences, which were not quite what she had hoped they would be. It was a matter of some delicacy.

As she disappeared Pop reminded the Brigadier of how he had said Miss Pilchester was a splendid organizer and all that.

The Brigadier was more than kind: 'Well, in her own sweet way I suppose she is. Fact is, I suppose, she's the only one who can spare the time. Nobody else has the time.'

That was it. Nobody had the time. In the crushing, rushing pressure of modern life nobody, even in the country, had the time.

A few moments later the Brigadier glanced hurriedly at his watch, saw it was after twelve o'clock and said he must rush back for a bite of cold. Pop begged him to come to the beer-tent for a quick snifter before he went but the Brigadier was firm. Nellie would be waiting. He was going to be adamant this time.

Pop, watching him depart with bemused admiration, re-

membered that word. The Brigadier had one shoe-lace miss-
ing and had replaced it with packing string. His hair badly
needed cutting at the back, and his shirt collar was, if anything, more frayed than before. But the word adamant shone
from him to remind Pop once again of all those wonderful
fellers who could use these startling words. He envied them
very much.

Going to the beer-tent he found that the bulldog of a judge
had arrived and was drinking with two members of the committee, Jack Woodley and Freda O'Connor. The judge was a
squat ebullient man in a bowler hat. With Woodley, a ruddy,
crude, thick-lipped man who was wearing a yellow waistcoat
under his hacking jacket, he kept up a constant braying duet,
swaying backwards and forwards, waving a pint mug of beer.
Woodley was evidently telling smoke-room stories, at the
same time gazing with rough interest at the notorious
O'Connor bosom, which protruded by several white marble
inches above a low yellow sweater. The coarser the stories the
more the O'Connor bosom seemed to like them. Like a
pair of bellows, its splendid heaving mass pumped air into
the hearty organ of her voice, setting the air about her ringing.

All three ignored Pop and he knew why. He and Ma hadn't
invited them to the cocktail party. Not caring, he said in a
loud voice, 'How's everybody? Fit as fleas?' as he went past
them. Nobody answered, but Pop didn't care. He believed in
treating everybody alike, fleas or no fleas.

Glass of beer in hand, he found a companion some moments
later in Sir George Bluff-Gore, who owned a large red-brick
Georgian mansion that was too expensive to keep up. He and
his wife somehow pigged it out in a keeper's cottage instead.
Bluff-Gore, yellowish, funereal, stiff, and despondent, had the

face of a pall bearer cramped by indigestion. He was not the sort of man you could slap on the back to wish him well.

Nevertheless Pop did so.

Bluff-Gore, recoiling with dejection, managed to say that it was nice of Larkin to invite him and Lady Rose to this cocktail party. They didn't get out much.

'More the merrier,' Pop said and then remembered that the Bluff-Gores had a daughter – Rosemary, he thought her name was – a big puddeny girl with sour eyes and a blonde fringe, whom he had sometimes seen riding at meetings or pony gymkhanas with Mariette. He wondered where she was; he hadn't seen her lately.

'Hope the daughter's coming too?' he said. 'Welcome.'

'Rosemary? Afraid not. Lives in London now.'

'Oh?' Pop said. 'Doing what? Working?'

With increasing gloom Bluff-Gore gazed at the grass of the beer-tent and thought of his only daughter, who had suddenly decided for some utterly unaccountable reason to give up a perfectly sound, happy, normal home to go and paint in Chelsea. It had practically broken her mother's heart; it was utterly unaccountable.

'Gone over to art,' he said.

It was as if he spoke of some old despicable enemy and Pop could only say he hoped it would turn out well.

Drinking again, deciding that art could only be some man or other that Rosemary had run off with, he suddenly switched the subject, charging the unready Bluff-Gore with a startling question.

'When are you going to sell Bluff Court, Sir George?'

Bluff-Gore looked white. For some moments he could find no suitable words with which to tell Pop that he had no intention of selling his house, Bluff Court, even though it was far too large to live in. Bluff Court had sixty rooms, an entire hamlet of barns, dairies, and stables, half a mile of greenhouses and potting sheds and an orangery where, for fifty years, no oranges had grown. You needed a hundred tons of coal to heat it every winter and eighteen gardeners to keep the place tidy and productive in summer. You needed to keep twenty servants to wait on you and another twenty to wait on them. It was dog eat dog. You couldn't get the servants anyway and you couldn't have afforded to pay them if you could.

But to give it up, to sell it, even though you hadn't a bean, was unthinkable. It was a monstrous idea; it simply couldn't be entertained. Among its miles of neglected beeches, elms, and oaks, Bluff Court must and would stand where it did. It might be that one day it would be possible to let it to one of those stockbroker chaps who played at farming, made colossal losses but in the end came out on the right side because they got it out of taxes. Everybody was doing it and it was all perfectly legitimate, they said. It just showed, of course, what the country was coming to. It was grim. No wonder everybody you met was worried stiff. The country was committing suicide. 'What makes you think I have any intention of selling Bluff Court?'

'Well, you don't live in the damn thing,' Pop said, straight as a bird, 'do you? And never will do if you ask me.'

Bluff-Gore indicated with funereal acidity that he was, in fact, not asking him.

'Damn silly,' Pop said. He started to say that it was like having a car you never rode in and then decided on a more illuminating, more contemporary metaphor and said: 'Like having a television set you never look at.'

The illustration was, however, lost on Sir George, who had no television set.

'There are certain aspects other than material', he said, 'that have to be borne in mind.'

Pop said he couldn't think for the life of him what they were, and Bluff-Gore looked at the perky, side-lined face with tolerant irony and an oysterish half-smile.

'You were not thinking of buying the place, by any chance, were you?'

'Course I was.' The gentry were, Pop thought, really half-dopes sometimes. 'What d'ye think I asked you for?'

The oysterish smile widened a little, still ironically tolerant, for the next question.

'And what would you do with it, may I ask?'

'Pull the flippin' thing down.' Pop gave one of his piercing, jolly shouts of laughter. 'What else d'ye think?'

'Good God.'

By now Bluff-Gore was whiter than ever. The eyes themselves had become oysters, opaque, sightless jellies, wet with shock, even with a glint of tears.

'Lot o' good scrap there,' Pop said. 'Make you a good offer.'

Bluff-Gore found himself quite incapable of speaking; he could only stare emptily and with increasing dejection at the grass of the beer-tent, as if mourning for some dear, unspoken departed.

'Cash,' Pop said. 'Ready as Freddy – why don't you think it over?'

Laughing again, he made a final expansive swing of his beer-mug, drawing froth, and left the speechless, sightless Bluff-Gore standing dismally alone.

Outside, in the meadow now gay with strung flags of yellow, scarlet, blue, and emerald, the tents and the marquees standing about the new green grass like white haystacks, Pop found the sun now shining brilliantly. Over by the river, well away from the ring, Mariette was having a practice canter. She had changed already into her yellow shirt and jodhpurs and her bare head was like a curly black kitten against the far blue sky. Mr Charlton was in attendance and suddenly Pop remembered the little matter of the baby. He supposed she wouldn't have to ride much longer and he wondered mildly if Mr Charlton knew. He'd forgotten about that.

Suddenly, from far across the meadow, he heard a rousing, familiar sound. It was Ma beating with a wooden spoon on a big jam-saucepan.

It was time to eat. It was hot in the midday sun and there was a scent of bruised grass in in the air.

'Perfick,' Pop thought. 'Going to be a stinger. Going to be a wonderful afternoon.'

*

All afternoon Mr Charlton watched Mariette taking part in the riding and jumping events she had chosen. Once again, as she took her pony faultlessly through the walk, trot, canter, and run, he could hardly believe in that astral delicious figure, yellow, fawn, and black on its bay pony. Impossible almost to believe that it was the girl who had undressed him on the billiard table, scratched the eyes out of Pauline Jackson, and worked with him in the strawberry field. Once again she looked so perfectly aristocratic that she might have been the niece of Lady Planson-Forbes and he had never been so happy in his life as he watched her.

Ma was happy too. Who wouldn't be? All the children were properly dressed for the occasion, wearing riding habits, jodhpurs, and proper riding caps, even though only Mariette and Montgomery were going to ride. Each of them went about sucking enormous pink and yellow ice-creams; and the twins, who took so much after Ma, had large crackling bags of popcorn and potato crisps.

Nor were there any flies on Ma. She was wearing a silk costume in very pale turquoise, with slightly darker perpendicular stripes. She had chosen a rather large dark blue straw hat that shaded her face nicely and, as the milliner had predicted, 'helped to balance her up a bit'. Her shoes were also blue, almost the colour of her hat, and her hair had been permed into stiffish little waves. The only thing that really bothered her was her turquoise rings. They had started to cut into her fingers again. She would have to have them off.

Beside her the Brigadier's sister looked, as she always did, in her beige shantung and pink cloche hat, like a clothes peg with a thimble perched on top of it.

'Not going in for this 'ere ladies' donkey Derby, are you?' Ma said. Her body quivered with resonant, jellying laughter.

An invitation to strip down to the bare bosom could hardly have brought less response from the sister of the Brigadier.

'I think Miss Pilchester's going in,' Ma said. 'Anyway Pop's trying to persuade her to.'

The ladies' donkey Derby was a late, inspired idea of Pop's. He had managed to persuade the committee that they owed it to him in return for the field. He had also found a silver cup. He had once bought it at a sale, thinking it would be nice to stand on the sideboard. It was engraved with the details of an angling competition, but Pop didn't think it mattered all that much.

While Ma wandered about with the children and Mr Charlton watched the various events, listening with pride every time the loudspeakers spoke the name of Miss Mariette Larkin, Pop was spending some time behind the beer-tent, trying to induce Miss Pilchester to ride in the donkey Derby.

'I honestly couldn't. It would be absolutely ghastly.'

'I thought you liked a bit o' fun?'

'I think you are trying to be very naughty.'

Irresistible though Miss Pilchester always found him, she could not help thinking that this afternoon, in the brilliant sun, Pop looked even more so. He was wearing a suit of small, smart brown-and-white checks, an orange-brown tie, and a new brown Edwardian cap. Like Ma, he compared very favourably with other people: with, for instance, the Brigadier, who was wearing a snuff-coloured sports jacket patched at the elbows with brown leather, his washed-out University tie, and a pair of crumpled corduroys the colour of a moulting stoat.

For the second or third time Pop urged Miss Pilchester to be a sport.

'Just one more rider to make up the seven.'

'Who else is riding? I have never even ridden a donkey in my life before.'

'All girls of your age.'

Miss Pilchester darted one of her rapid glances at Pop. The cast of suspicion died in her eye as she saw the brown new cap. How well it suited him.

'What about that time I took you home in the Rolls?'

'What about it?'

'Best kiss I've had for a long time.'

'You make me feel shy!' Miss Pilchester said.

'Beauty,' Pop said. 'Haven't been able to forget it.'

Miss Pilchester hadn't been able to forget it either; she had even wondered if it might ever be repeated.

'I admit it was far from unpleasant, but what has it to do with the donkey Derby?'

Pop started to caress the outer rim of Miss Pilchester's thigh.

With upsurgent alarm Miss Pilchester felt an investigating finger press a suspender button.

'People will be looking!'

'Coming to the cocktail party?'

'I think so. Yes, I am.'

'Repeat performance tonight at the cocktail party. Promise.'

'I know those promises. They're like pie-crust!'

At four o'clock Miss Pilchester was ready to ride in the ladies' donkey Derby.

A quarter of an hour before that Montgomery and Mr Charlton had ridden in the men's donkey Derby. Most of the donkeys, including Mr Charlton's, had had to be started with carrots and the race had been won by a pale sagacious animal named Whiskey Johnny, who didn't need any carrots. Mr Charlton had ridden three yards and then fallen off. His mount had instantly bolted, ending up in stirring style far beyond the tea-tent, by the river, where already a few lovers, bored by the events and stimulated by a warm afternoon of entrancing golden air, were embracing in the long grasses by the bank, profitably dreaming out the day in a world of rising fish, wild irises, and expanding water-lily blooms.

When Pop went to collect the animal, which was called Jasmine, he found it staring with detached interest at a soldier and a passionate, well-formed young blonde, both of whom were oblivious, in the grasses, of the presence of watchers. Jasmine, Pop thought, seemed so interested in what was going on that after being led away some paces she turned, pricked up her ears and looked around, rather as if she wanted to come back and see it all again.

After all this Pop selected Jasmine for Miss Pilchester to ride. The animal stood dangerously still at the starting point, in stubborn suspense, while Pop gave earnest ante-post advice to Miss Pilchester, who sat astride.

'Hang on with your knees. Don't let go. Hang on tight. Like grim death.'

Miss Pilchester, already looking like grim death, gave a hasty glance round at the other competitors, dismayed to find them all young, effervescent girls of sixteen or seventeen. She herself felt neither young nor effervescent and the donkey was horribly hairy underneath her calves.

'Don't mind them, Edith. Don't look at them. Look straight ahead – straight as you can go. Hang on like grim death.'

Miss Pilchester became vaguely aware of carrots, in orange arcs, being waved in all directions. A few animals trotted indifferently up the track, between shrieking, cheering rows of spectators. One trotted at incautious speed for thirty yards or so and then, as if inexplicably bored about something, turned and came back. Another sidled to the side of the track and leaned against a post, allowing itself to be stroked by various children, including Victoria and the twins. Two girls fell off, screaming, and there were gay momentary glimpses of black and apricot lingerie.

Jasmine stood fast. 'Git up, old gal!' Pop said, and started to push her. 'Git up there, Jasmine!' Pop put his weight against her rump and heaved. Nothing happened, and it seemed as if Jasmine had sunk her feet into the ground.

It was all absolutely ghastly, Miss Pilchester was just thinking when over the loudspeaker a voice started up an announcement about Anne Fitzgerald, aged three, who had lost her mother. Would Mrs Fitzgerald please –

The loudspeaker gave a few snappy barks. Jasmine cocked her ears and broke through with frenzy the final waving arcs of carrots, leaving Pop on the ground and everybody scattered.

Miss Pilchester, as Pop had so earnestly and correctly advised, hung on firmly and desperately with her knees, just like grim death, and in thirty seconds Jasmine was back at the river, once more staring into the world of grasses, water-lilies, irises, and a soldier's summer love.

Half-dismounting, half-falling, a dishevelled and demoralized Miss Pilchester stood staring too. It was all absolutely and utterly ghastly and it only made things worse when the soldier, disturbed in the middle of his technique, looked up calmly and said:

'Why don't you go away, Ma? Both of you. You *and* your sister.'

8

POP, uncertain as to quite who had been invited to the party and who had not, spent most of the rest of the afternoon hailing odd acquaintances, generously clapping them on the back, and saying: 'See you at eight o'clock. See you at the party.' The result was that by half past eight the billiard-room was a clamorous, fighting mass of fifty or sixty people, one half of whom had never received a formal invitation.

'I never thought we asked this lot,' Ma said. 'Hardly enough stuff to go round –'

'Let 'em all come!' Pop said.

The billiard-room was the perfick place, he thought, for having the party. The billiard table, covered over by trestle table boards and then with a big white cloth, was just the thing for the eats, the champagne, and the glasses. One of the doors led back into the house, in case people wanted to pop upstairs, and the other into the garden, so that those who felt inclined could dodge out and take the air.

Through the thickest fog of smoke Pop had ever seen outside a smoking concert he and Ma, helped by Mariette, Mr Charlton, and Montgomery, served food, poured out champagne, and handed glasses round. Every now and then people collided with each other in the crowded fog and a glass went smashing to the floor. Nobody seemed to care about this and Ma was glad the glasses had been hired from caterers. That was another brilliant idea of Mr Charlton's.

Now and then someone, almost always someone he hardly knew, came up to Pop, squeezed his elbow, and said, 'Damn good party, Larkin, old boy. Going well,' so that Pop felt very pleased. Ma too moved everywhere with genial expansiveness. In the crowd she seemed larger than ever, so that whenever she moved her huge body from one spot to another a large open vacuum was formed.

In one of these spaces, alongside a wall, Pop found the two Miss Barnwells, Effie and Edna, who, to his infinite pain and surprise, had no crumb or glass between them. The Miss Barnwells, who were thinking of applying for National Assistance because times were so bad, were two genteel freckled little ladies, daughters of an Indian civil servant, who had been born in Delhi. Among other things they kept bees and their little yellow faces, crowded with freckles, looked as if they were regularly and thoroughly stung all over.

'Nothing to eat? Nothing to drink?'

Pop could hardly believe it; he was shocked.

'We were just contemplating.'

'Contemplate my foot,' Pop said. 'I'll get you a glass o' champagne.'

'No, no,' they said. 'Nothing at all like that.'

'Terrible,' Pop said. 'Nobody looking after you. I'll get you a sandwich.'

Coming back a moment or two later with a plate of Ma's delicious buttery ham sandwiches, he returned to the painful subject of the Miss Barnwells and their having nothing to drink at all.

'Glass o' beer? Drop o' cider? Glass o' port?'

'No, no. No, thank you. We are quite happy.'

'Have a Ma Chérie.'

The air seemed to light up with infinite twinkling freckles.

'What is a Ma Chérie?'

Ma Chérie was hardly, Pop thought, a drink at all. It was simply sherry, soda, and a dash of something or other, he could never remember quite what. It was nothing like Red Bull or Rolls-Royce or Chauffeur, the good ones.

'Soda with flavouring,' he said.

'That sounds quite nice. Perhaps we might have two of –'

Pop was away, pushing through the foggy crowd to the living-room, where he presently mixed two Ma Chéries, double strength, adding an extra dash of brandy to hold the feeble things together.

'There you are. Knock that back.'

The Miss Barnwells, who hardly ever had much lunch on Saturdays, took their glasses, chewing rapidly, and thanked him. The air danced with freckles. He was, they said, infinitely kind.

'I'll keep 'em topped up,' Pop said.

A moment later a firm gentle hand fixed itself to his elbow and drew him away.

'Mr Larkin, isn't it?'

A tallish lady in a small grey tweed hat with a peacock feather in it smiled at him over a piece of cheese toast and a glass of champagne.

'Lady Bluff-Gore. You remember?'

Pop remembered; they had met occasionally at village Christmas socials.

'Ah, yes,' Pop said. 'Lady Rose.'

'Afraid we don't run across each other very often.'

She smiled again; her ivory teeth were remarkably long and large.

'I hear you made an interesting suggestion to my husband this afternoon.'

'Oh! about the house? That's right. Time it was pulled down.'

'So I heard.'

All afternoon she had been thinking what an interesting suggestion it was to pull the house down. She had so long wanted to pull it down herself.

'Who wants these old places?' Pop said.

Who indeed? she thought. She had so often longed to pull hers down, and all the miles of silly greenhouses, unused stables, and draughty barns. Perhaps if it were pulled down, she thought, they might have a little money in the bank instead of living on overdrafts. Perhaps Rosemary would come back. Perhaps they could really live in comfort for a change.

'Would it be too much to ask what you feel it's worth?'

'Could take a squint at it tomorrow,' Pop said, 'and let you know.'

Nothing like striking the iron while it was hot, Pop thought. That's how he liked to do things. In a couple of hours he could get a rough idea what bricks, tiles, doors, flooring, and hard core he would get out of it. In two shakes he could be on the blower to Freddy Fox and do a deal with Freddy.

'Yes, I'll take a squint at it –'

'Do you suppose – could we talk elsewhere?' she said. Her voice was quiet. 'It's a little public here.'

Elsewhere, at Pop's suggestion, was under the walnut tree. The evening was overcast and humid, with a feeling of coming rain. Cuckoos were still calling across the fields in their late bubbling voices and a few people were wandering among Ma's flower-beds, taking the air.

'You see it wouldn't be at all an easy business to persuade my husband.'

'No?'

'Not at all an easy man.'

Pop didn't doubt it at all.

'All the same I think I might persuade him.'

If he could persuade Miss Pilchester to ride the donkey, Pop thought, it ought to be possible to persuade Bluff-Gore to do a little thing like pulling a mansion down. Nothing to it. Perhaps by much the same process too?

'It's just a thought,' she said, 'but supposing I did?'

'Don't get it,' Pop said.

'Mightn't it be an idea to come to some little arrangement? You and I?'

Women were clever, Pop thought. That showed you how clever women were. All the same under their skins. He snagged on now. Lady Five Per Cent he would call her now.

'I get you,' Pop said.

'Good. Shall I let you know when we might have another little talk?'

Back in the smoky, clamorous fog he discovered the Miss Barnwells gazing at empty glasses. How had they liked the Ma Chérie? Quite delicious, they thought; and he went away to get them more.

In the comparative quiet of the sitting-room, where it was getting dusk, he got the impression that the entire billiard-room would, at any moment, blow up behind him. The place was a whirring dynamo, rapidly running hot.

'And what about me?'

It was Miss Pilchester, furtive against the Spanish galleon. Another one come to collect her interest, Pop supposed.

'Having a nice time?'

'It'll be nicer when you've kept your promise.'

Might as well get it over, Pop thought.

'Lovely party. Such luck with the weather. Best gymkhana we've ever had.'

Pop put down the two Ma Chéries and braced himself. Miss

Pilchester simply didn't know how to hold herself for the act of kissing and Pop seized her like a sheaf of corn. There was a momentary bony stir of corsets and Miss Pilchester gave a short palpitating sigh. She had determined, this time, to give everything she'd got.

For all the velvet artistry he put into it Pop could make little impression on lips so well fortified with teeth that he felt they might at any moment crack like walnuts underneath the strain.

'Thanks. That was just what the doctor ordered. Time for one more?'

'Last one,' Pop said. 'Must get back to the party.'

With thrilling silence Miss Pilchester gave everything she'd got for the second time. It was almost too much for Pop, who throughout the kiss was wondering if, after all, he might indulge in a firework or two. Finally Miss Pilchester broke away, gazing wildly up at him.

'And in case I don't get another chance of seeing you alone again, thanks for everything. Marvellous day. All your doing. Simply wouldn't have been anything without you. Best gymkhana we've ever had. And this party. Made me very happy.'

The length of the speech suddenly seemed to take away the rest of her capacity for calm. She gave something like a sob, patted Pop's cheek, and rushed hurriedly away and upstairs, brushing past two women already on their way up. Once more she had forgotten to say how absolutely ghastly everything was.

'You simply must see the polly,' one woman was saying. 'Purple and yellow tiles with big blue hollyhocks coming out the top. And pink nymphs on the bath mirror.'

'Oh! God!' Miss Pilchester said.

Taking the two Ma Chéries back to the Miss Barnwells Pop

found them laughing merrily, chewing at their seventh ham sandwich.

'Going positively to drag you away if you'll let me.'

The longest, slimmest, coolest hand Pop had ever touched suddenly came and took him sinuously away from the munching Miss Barnwells, now eagerly sipping their second Ma Chéries.

'They tell me you practically organized this whole bun-fight single-handed.'

A tall aristocratically fair girl, so fair that her hair was almost barley-white, with a figure like a reed and enormous pellucid olive eyes, had Pop so transfixed that, for a moment, he was almost unnerved. He had never seen her, or anyone like her, before.

'The thing positively went like a bomb.'

The cool, long hand still held his own. The large pale eyes, languidly swimming, washed over him an endless stream of softer and softer glances.

'And this party. What a slam.'

Her dress was pure clear primrose, with a long V-neck. She wore long transparent earrings that swung about her long neck like dewy pendulums.

'Going to have a party of my own next week. Say you'll come.'

Pop, who had so far not spoken a word, murmured something about he'd love to, trying at the same time to decide where and when he'd seen this unheralded vision before, deciding finally that he never had.

'Gorgeous party. Do you dance at all?'

'Used to fling 'em up a bit at one time.'

'Scream.'

She laughed on clear bell-like notes.

'My dear. Absolute scream.'

Bewitched, Pop again had nothing to say. A vacuum left by Ma, three or four feet away from him, made him feel quite naked before it filled up again.

'That donkey ride, they tell me, was your idea. Blistering success.'

Pop, with a certain touch of pride, admitted it.

'The seven foolish virgins. Scream. Couldn't stop laughing. Practically needed changing –'

Again she laughed on pure bell-like notes, the dewy earrings dancing.

'Just what it needed. They can be absolute stinkers, gymkhanas, don't you think? Everybody jog-trotting round. Fond mothers biting lips because little Waffles doesn't win the trotting on Pretty Boy. Oh! absolute stinkers.'

She held him captured with moist splendid eyes.

'But you thought of the virgins. That was the stroke. Absolute genius. Absolute scream, the virgins.'

She suddenly gave Pop what he thought was a fleeting sporting wink.

'So few, after all, aren't there?'

To Pop it now began to seem that he might have met, under the sheer primrose sheath, the dancing earrings, the aristocratic voice, and the shining languid eyes, a character something after his own heart and kind.

'But seriously, dear man, what I came to say was this. My name's Angela Snow. Emhurst Valley. We've got one of these pony-trots coming off in August – what say you come over and bring the donkey outfit and make that one go with a bang?'

The word bang made Pop remember something. It was, he thought, the one thing needed to make the day a perfick one.

'Like fireworks?'

'Love 'em. Adore 'em.'

'Stay here,' Pop said, 'while I fetch you a drop more champagne.' He started to struggle through the smoky screen hemming him in on all sides and then remembered something and came back to her. 'Or a cocktail? Rather have a cocktail?'

'Adore one. Just what I need.'

'This way.'

He started to lead the way out to the sitting-room, but half way he was stopped by Mr Charlton and Mariette, who said:

'Pop, Charley has something he'd like to say to you.'

'Not now,' Pop said. 'Busy now.'

'It's terribly important. It's something he's *got* to ask you.'

Mr Charlton looked unexpectedly strained and tense. Must have found out about the baby, Pop supposed. Pity.

'Be back in five minutes,' he said and followed the tall, reedy, primrose figure into the sitting-room.

There, over his Spanish galleon, he asked the dewy, languid girl which she would rather have – Rolls-Royce, Red Bull, or Chauffeur. Red Bull was the blinder, he said.

'Red Bull then, dear,' she said. 'What names they give them nowadays.'

Pop mixed two double Red Bulls and in the falling twilight the elegant Angela Snow knocked hers back with the coolest speed, like a man.

'One more of these, dear boy, and I'm ready.'

Pop was ready too. Ten minutes later the first firework went off like a bomb under Ma, who showed hardly any sign of disturbance at all. The two ladies who had been to investigate Ma's impossible bathroom met a Roman Candle on the stairs. The tall reedy girl put two jumping crackers under the

Brigadier's sister and another under Sir George Bluff-Gore. Ma started laughing like a jelly and Pop put a Mighty Atom under the billiard table where it set the glasses ringing like a xylophone. The two Miss Barnwells started giggling uncontrollably and said it reminded them of a pujah in Delhi and Miss Pilchester was heard saying she knew this would happen and that it was absolutely ghastly and she'd hide under the stairs. People started running from the smoky house into the garden, where the tall, languid girl had a big fizzing Catherine Wheel already going on the walnut tree and was now getting ready to put a Roman Candle as near as she could without killing him under a man named Jack Farley, who was a complete slob and had tried to pinch her three times in the tea-tent early in the afternoon. A few rockets started shooting up from empty champagne bottles into a sky now summerily dark, cuckoo-less, and completely canopied with cloud. Pop did what he had so long wanted to do and put a beauty under Miss Pilchester, who started shrieking she was burned. Upstairs Primrose, Victoria, and the twins hung out of the bedroom windows shouting, laughing, and eating the day's last ice-cream, potato crisps, and apple-tart. In the middle of it all Mariette and Mr Charlton tried once again, with little success, to speak with Pop, who was running about the flower beds waving a Golden Rain, calling like a Red Indian, happy as a boy. When finally Pop had thrown the Golden Rain over a damson tree Mr Charlton said:

'Pop, I want to speak to you. Ma says I can marry Mariette if you'll let her –'

'Perfick,' Pop said. 'Let her? – course I'll let her.'

The tall, willowy girl was everywhere, selecting victims. The sky was comet-bright with sprays of silver stars, rockets, and Golden Rain. A Roman Candle went off with shattering concussion behind the walnut tree and Mr Charlton begged of Pop:

'Pop, Ma says if you agree will you announce it? She says now's the perfect time.'

'Perfick it is an' all,' Pop said. 'Never thought of that.'

A quarter of an hour later Pop was standing on a chair outside the billiard-room, announcing to the gathered guests, in the smoky garden, with a touch of imperial pride in his voice, together with a certain sadness, that Mr Charlton was going to marry his daughter Mariette and had everybody got their glasses filled?

'Give you the toast!' he called into the smoky summer air. 'Charley and Mariette.'

As he lifted his glass a stunning explosion split the air, knocking him yards backwards.

'One for his nob!' Mr Charlton shouted.

'What Paddy shot at!' Ma screamed and started choking in helpless laughter.

It was the last devastating Roman Candle of the cool, tall, primrose girl.

'Quite perfect,' she said.

9

WHEN it was all over, and even television had closed down, Ma and Pop sat alone in the kitchen, Ma now and then shaking all over as she remembered the donkeys, Miss Pilchester, and the way Pop had been blown flat on his back by the Roman Candle.

'Nothing at all to eat?' Pop inquired.

'Think there's another apple-tart,' Ma said and got up to get it from the fridge. The apple-tart was large and puffy, with white castor sugar sprinkled on its lid of crust. With it Ma brought two plates, a knife and, out of sheer habit, the bottle of ketchup. 'By the way, who was that girl in the yellow dress? She was a spark.'

'Never seen her in me life. Somebody said her father was a judge.'

'Oh?' Ma said. 'Well, I suppose there's a throw-back in every family.'

Pop cut two six-inch slices of pie. He gave one to Ma, and then started to eat the other in his fingers, at the same time ignoring, much to Ma's surprise, the bottle of ketchup.

'Don't you want no ketchup?'

'Gone off ketchup a bit,' Pop said.

'Oh?' Ma said. 'How's that?'

'Makes everything taste the same.'

Ma, who thought this was odd, went on to say what about port?

'Don't say you've gone off port as well.'

'No,' Pop said. 'Just got some more in. Started to order it in two-gallon jars now.'

He got up, found the jar of port under the stairs and poured out two nice big glasses, inquiring at the same time where Mr Charlton and Mariette were?

'Having a quiet few minutes in the sitting-room.'

Pop said it was very nice about Mr Charlton and Mariette and had Mr Charlton found out about the baby?

'She's not going to have a baby now,' Ma said. 'False alarm.'

'Jolly good,' Pop said. 'Perfick.'

Ma sat meditatively fingering her turquoise rings, which seemed to be getting tighter every day, while Pop listened to the sound of the first gentle summery feathers of rain on earth and leaves as it came through the open kitchen door.

'I am though,' Ma said.

Pop looked mildly, though not disagreeably, surprised.

'How did that happen then?'

'*How*? What do you mean, *how*?'

Pop said he meant when did it all date back to?

'That night in the bluebell wood,' Ma said. 'Just before Mister Charlton came. You said you thought there was a wild duck's nest up there and we went to have a look.'

'That night?' Pop said. 'I never even thought –'

'You don't know your own strength,' Ma said. 'Have some more apple-tart. Pass the ketchup.'

Pop cut himself another biggish slice of apple-tart. Ma, he noticed, hadn't quite finished hers. She was always a slow eater. She was still fingering her turquoise rings, as if for some reason she was engaged in thinking, though Pop couldn't imagine what about, unless it was the baby.

The turquoise rings, however, put a thought into his own mind, and he gave a short soft laugh or two, no louder than the summery feathers of rain.

'If this lark goes on much longer', he said, 'you and me'll have to get married as well.'

Ma said she thought it wouldn't be a bad idea perhaps.

'I've got to have my rings cut off again anyway,' she said. 'We might as well do it then.'

For some moments Pop sat in complete silence, still listening to the rain and wondering about the baby and if Ma wanted a boy and what names they would pick for it when it came.

Ma sat wondering too, mostly about what it would be like to be married. She couldn't imagine at all.

Eventually Pop spoke. 'Thought up any names for it?' he said.

'It?' Ma said. 'I've got a funny feeling it might be twins.'

'Marvellous. Perfick,' Pop said.

Ma, who had in fact thought a very great deal about names, went on to say that if it did turn out to be just a boy, which she hoped it wouldn't, or just a girl, what about Orlando and Rosalind? – out of that play they saw on television the other night? A very nice play.

Pop said he thought they were jolly good names, just the sort of names he liked. And what if it was twins?

'Well,' Ma said, 'I've been thinking. If it's girls I thought of Lucinda and Clorinda. I think they're very nice. Or if it's boys I wouldn't say no to Nelson and Rodney. They were admirals.'

'Not so bad,' Pop said. 'I like Lucinda.'

The rain was falling a little faster now, though still softly, the dampness bringing out of the air the last lingering smell of firework smoke. At one time the house had seemed full of the stench of gunpowder.

'Couldn't very well make it a double wedding, I suppose, could we?' Ma said.

'Might ask Mister Charlton.'

'Why Mister Charlton?'

'He knows about things. Look what he knew about the party.'

Pop had just finished his second slice of apple-pie and was vaguely wondering about a third – there wasn't so much of it left and it was a pity to let it go begging – when Mr Charlton and Mariette came in from the sitting-room. He said how glad he was to see them and how he could congratulate them now it was quieter. He said he and Ma weren't half glad about things and that it didn't seem five minutes since Mister Charlton had arrived.

'How about a glass of port, you two?'

While he was pouring out two more nice big glasses of port he couldn't help thinking how pretty Mariette looked in her black, semi-fitting cocktail dress with its white cuffs, collar, and belt. He hoped all the girls would take after Ma. He thought too how nice it was about Mariette and the baby – just as well to start with a clean sheet about these things.

'Well, cheers,' he said. 'God bless,' and with a sudden affectionate impulse got up and kissed Mariette. 'Couldn't be more perfick.'

Ma, who said she wasn't going to be left out, then got up and kissed both Mariette and Mr Charlton; and then Mr Charlton and Pop shook hands.

'Got a bit of news of our own now,' Pop said. 'Shall we tell them, Ma?'

'You tell them.'

'Well,' Pop said, 'we thought we'd get married too. Ma's going to have another baby.'

Mr Charlton, who only a month before would have been more than startled by this announcement, didn't turn a hair.

Nor did Mariette seem unduly perturbed. The only thing that suddenly occurred to Mr Charlton was that this was a time when it was essential, if ever, to use his loaf.

'Now wait a minute,' he said, 'this wants thinking about.'

'There you are, Ma,' Pop said. 'I told you.'

'Why does it want thinking about?' Ma said.

Mr Charlton took a thoughtful sip of port.

'I was thinking of the tax situation,' he said. 'You see, it actually doesn't pay to get married. It actually pays to live in –'

He was about to say 'sin' but abruptly checked himself, too late to prevent Ma, however, from being a little upset.

'Don't use that word,' she said severely. 'I know what you were going to say.'

Mr Charlton apologized and said what he really meant was that if he were them he'd keep the *status quo*. This was the first time Pop had ever heard such astonishing un-English words used under his own roof, but it meant more marks for Mr Charlton. Ma, forgetting that she had been very nearly outraged a moment before, could only look on in silent, fervent admiration.

'Quite happy as we are, I suppose, eh, Ma?' Pop said. 'Nothing to worry about?'

Not that she could think of, Ma said.

'All right. Let's go on in the old sweet way.'

Mr Charlton agreed.

'By keeping to the old way,' Mr Charlton said, 'you'll be better off when the time comes.'

'When what time comes?' Pop said. 'For what?'

'To pay your tax,' Mr Charlton said. 'It's bound to catch up some day.'

'That's what you think!' Pop said.

'I'm afraid they'll take notice of the Rolls. They're bound to say –'

'That old thing?' Pop said. 'Never. Took it for a debt!'

Suddenly Pop started laughing as heartily as Ma had done when the girl in the yellow dress had blown him off the chair with the Roman Candle.

Ma laughed piercingly too and said: 'Oh! that reminds me. Are you going back to that office?'

'That's right, Charley,' Pop said. 'Are you ever going back to that lark?'

Mr Charlton, thoughtful again, said he supposed if he didn't go back he'd lose his pension.

The word pension made Pop laugh even more than the idea of the tax lark. 'You mean sit on your backside for forty years and then collect four pounds a week that's worth only two and 'll only buy half as much anyway?' He urged Mr Charlton to use his loaf. Mr Charlton could not help thinking that it was high time he did. 'I tell you what,' Pop said. 'I'll be doing a nice little demolition job very soon. Some very good stuff. Big mansion. What say we pick the best out and build you and Mariette a bungalow in the medder, near the bluebell wood?'

'Oh! wonderful, wonderful, Pop!' Mariette said and, with eyes impulsively dancing, came to kiss his face and lips and hair, so that Mr Charlton knew that there was, really, nothing more to say.

'Well, that's it then,' Pop said. 'Perfick. Now who says one more glass o' port? And then we go to bed.'

He was intensely looking forward to going to bed. It would top it all up to have a cigar and watch Ma get into the transparent nylon nightgown.

'Yes: time to get a little beauty sleep,' Ma said.

Pop poured four more nice big glasses of port, saying at the same time how glad he was about the rain. They could do with the rain. It was just what the cherries, the plums, and the apples wanted now.

'Shall you come cherry-picking too?' Mariette said to Mr Charlton, but in answer he could only look at her olive skin, the dark shining eyes, the kittenish hair, and the firm young breasts with silent fascination.

Some moments later Pop took his glass of port to the kitchen door, staring out at the summer darkness and the rain. Mr Charlton felt an impulse to join him and stood there staring too, thinking of how spring had passed, how quickly the buds of May had gone, and how everything, now, had blossomed into full, high summer.

'Listen,' Pop said. 'Perfick.'

Everybody listened; and in the dark air there was the sound of nightingales.

MORE ABOUT PENGUINS
AND PELICANS

For further information about books available from Penguins please write to Dept EP, Penguin Books Ltd, Harmondsworth, Middlesex UB7 0DA.

In the U.S.A.: For a complete list of books available from Penguins in the United States write to Dept CS, Penguin Books, 625 Madison Avenue, New York, New York 10022.

In Canada: For a complete list of books available from Penguins in Canada write to Penguin Books Canada Ltd, 2801 John Street, Markham, Ontario L3R 1B4.

In Australia: For a complete list of books available from Penguins in Australia write to the Marketing Department, Penguin Books Australia Ltd, P.O. Box 257, Ringwood, Victoria 3134.

In New Zealand: For a complete list of books available from Penguins in New Zealand write to the Marketing Department, Penguin Books (NZ) Ltd, P.O. Box 4019, Auckland 10.

H. E. Bates's Best-selling 'Larkin' Books

A Breath of French Air

They're here again – the indestructible Larkins; this time, with Baby Oscar, the Rolls, and Ma's unmarried passport, they're off to France. And with H. E. Bates, you may be sure, there's no French without tears of laughter.

When the Green Woods Laugh

In the third of the Larkin novels. H. E. Bates makes the Dragon's Blood and the double scotches hit with no less impact than they did in *The Darling Buds of May*. For the full Larkin orchestra is back on the rural fiddle, and (with Angela Snow around) the Brigadier may be too old to ride but he's young enough to fall. 'Pa is as sexy, genial, generous, and boozy as ever. Ma is a worthy match for him in all these qualities' – *The Times*

Oh! To Be in England

Are you taking life too seriously?
What you need is a dose of *Oh! To Be in England* – another splendid thighs-breasts-and-buttercups frolic though the Merrie England of the sixties with the thirsty, happy, lusty, quite uninhibited and now rightly famous junk-dealing family of Larkins.

A Little of What You Fancy

Things may be going well for Primrose Larkin, but they are far less 'perfick' for Pa Larkin. For in this, the fifth delightful story of the Larkin family, Pa has a mild heart attack. Even though the cunning Ma sends a succession of women up to his bedroom to tempt him back to health, he takes a long time to recover . . .